Clear Christmas

PAUL E. WOOTTEN

Grebey Creek Publishing
Lakewood Ranch, Florida USA

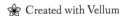 Created with Vellum

PART ONE

CHAPTER ONE

I HEAR A VOICE BUT AM NOT SURE WHERE IT'S COMING from. Or if it's even real.

The voice is talking about a place called Flanagan Furniture. The name is familiar, or maybe not. I say it aloud. Slowly. "Flan-a-gan." It feels natural rolling off my tongue.

"That's right, Neal." The voice is louder now. Closer. Male. "You do remember." Then he says something else, but his voice fades away as he's speaking. "I wish you were back, because..."

The whiteness returns. I fight it, because it makes me sad, but it comes anyway. I sleep and wake up. Then sleep some more. Two people come and get me out of the chair. Who they are, I don't know. The large black one smiles and rubs my arm. The smaller one doesn't smile or talk. And he smells like something. A few minutes later, we are in the bright sunshine, and I begin to remember.

"I coached Stephanie's softball team when she was seven. We went nine-and-two. She pitched and played second base."

We're walking now, around a circular track. There are other people out here, most in wheelchairs with their heads bowed. They should take better care of themselves.

"Was she good?" the black one asks.

I have no idea what he's talking about, so I don't answer. I concentrate on walking. And the space around me. It's very nice. There are shade trees like at Grandmother Flanagan's house in the country.

"She grows the best tomatoes," I say.

"Who, Neal? Your daughter?"

"She makes tomato and mayonnaise sandwiches. And pepper. There's always pepper on them."

"I love tomatoes," the white one says. He smells bad, like he needs deodorant.

"My God, you stink," I say, because he does.

He laughs. "Tell you what then, buddy. I'll go take my smoke break. You know your way around the track just fine without me."

The white one leaves, then the black one says, "I'm going inside, Neal. I'll come back for you later."

Now I'm alone. Walking. It feels good. The sun is warm. My legs feel strong. When I get warmed up maybe I'll run a little. I like running. I look around and spot Rosalie. She's seated on a bench under a palm tree. I smile as I approach.

"Rosie."

She doesn't answer. Doesn't look up. I sit down next to her and take her hand.

"Rosalie, remember when we went to Chicago for the half-marathon last year?"

Rosalie still doesn't answer, and it's starting to concern me. I squeeze her hand, just a little bit, but she pulls it away, tells me her name is Lillian, and calls me a fresh son-of-a-bitch.

CHAPTER TWO

I LIKE MORNING BEST. ESPECIALLY BEFORE THE SUN comes up. The hallway is quiet and, except for a couple of elderly people dozing in wheelchairs, empty. I sit across from a desk where a young man watches a basketball game on a computer screen. He's very careful to hide it when he hears anyone coming.

"Who's winning?" I ask.

He grins. "Heat beating the Celtics. It's a replay from last night. You a fan?"

"Of what?"

"The NBA."

"Oh, yes, I'm a big Nate Thurmond fan."

The guy's face twists in confusion. He must not be as big a fan as he claims, or he would know Nate Thurmond. He's too embarrassed to admit it, though, so he goes back to watching the game until a nurse comes to the counter.

"Terrell in Room 109, her husband is coming to get her for the weekend. I need a leave form," she says.

The guy at the desk looks confused again.

"Right there." The nurse points to a tray full of paper.

The guy pulls out a sheet and hands it to her. She heads back down the hall.

WHEN I WAKE up there's a glimmer of light coming through the windows behind the desk where the people sit. It's empty, the desk. All four chairs are empty. The man who watches basketball is gone, too. I get up, stretch to loosen the kinks in my knees and shoulders, and approach the counter. I glance around, then reach into a tray full of paper, pull out a sheet, and look at it.

Resident Leave Form.

I fold it and place it in my pocket.

THE FOLDER in the nightstand is full of pictures.

There's Rosalie. Disney World, 1978. We drove over for the day. Tickets were $6.50 each, a ridiculous amount, but I didn't complain. Rosalie had wanted to go to Disney World since the park opened back in '71. There's a little girl in the picture, too, wearing Mickey Mouse ears. I wrack my brain but don't recall her. I flip the picture over and see Rosalie's familiar handwriting.

Rosalie and Stephanie. Daddy wouldn't let us take his picture.

Daddy? I had no recollection that Rosie's father came along. It would be just like him, though. Probably hung back so we'd pay for his ticket, too. I'm thrifty, but compared to Hank Wainwright... Stephanie? Is she one of Rosalie's nieces? That must be right...

WHO ARE THESE PEOPLE?

The room is packed with them. The one sitting next to me, a woman, is snoring. I elbow her, but it doesn't help.

There are people putting up a Christmas tree. They're laughing. Then one comes to me and holds out her hand.

"Neal, do you want to hang an ornament?"

"Let Rosalie do it," I answer, because Rosalie always decorates the tree. The lady goes away, and the whiteness descends.

JINGLE BELLS!

It's one of my favorites, so I join in. There's a Christmas tree in the center of the room. It's large and beautifully decorated. Some of the people seated around me are singing along. Others sit with heads down and hands in their laps. Probably Jewish. We Christians tend to push Christmas on them. The singing makes me feel good, so I stand up. A young blonde girl I don't know comes over and takes my hand. She's pretty, so I let her lead me to the front of the room.

"You have a beautiful voice, Neal," she says. I thank her.

The song ends and we move onto *Santa Claus is Coming to Town*. Another favorite. Stephanie sings this one almost nonstop in the weeks leading up to Christmas. We spoil Stephanie. Rosalie knows it and I know it. She gets way more toys than any little girl should, just one benefit of being an only child.

"Where's Stephanie?" I ask the girl who brought me up front.

"Who is Stephanie?"

I bristle at the question. She should know exactly who Stephanie is. Perhaps she's new to the family, a beau of one of Rosie's kid brothers, maybe.

"My daughter," I answer patiently. "She's seven this year. Rosie and I don't know how much longer she'll believe in Santa, so we want this to be an extra special Christmas." I lean closer and whisper. "We got her an Easy-Bake Oven."

The girl claps her hands joyously. "I had one of those when I was seven! Stephanie will love it!"

The song comes to an end and the girl asks what song I want to sing next. I think about it but just don't know which...

CHAPTER THREE

"Neal, it's your grandson, Michael. Do you want to talk to him?"

I turn away from the TV. One of the women who works at this place is holding a cellphone.

"Of course, I do," I answer, getting to my feet. The woman who works here hands me the phone.

"Hi, Michael!"

"Hi, Grandpa. How are you?"

"Very well. I just finished breakfast and now I'm watching *The Price is Right*. It's the damndest thing, Michael. They just gave away a car that cost twenty-six grand. The first house Rosalie and I bought cost twenty-four-nine."

Michael laughs. It sounds nice.

"Tell me what's new with you," I say.

"I finished my classes, Grandpa. Graduation was last Saturday. I wish you could've been there."

"Wonderful! Congratulations, Michael. I wish I could've been there, too. Grandma must've forgotten to tell me it was last weekend. Is she still up there with you and your Mom and Dad?"

"Grandpa, Grandma is... no, she's not. I'm not at Mom and Dad's either. I'm in my apartment in Baltimore."

"Are kids your age allowed to have apartments now?"

Michael laughs that nice laugh again. "Grandpa, I'm twenty-two. I just finished college. I haven't found a job yet, though." The merriment of his laugh is gone. "I've sent out lots of resumes so something's going to happen sooner or later. I'm substitute teaching to make ends meet."

"Don't give up," I say, trying to sound encouraging. "You've got Flanagan blood running through your veins. That should be enough to get... you know, Michael, you could always come to Florida and work at the factory. I would love to make a place for you there. It'll be yours one day, you know."

The line grows quiet. I worry that I've stepped on his toes by suggesting that he become part of the family business, so I change the subject.

"Do you want to talk to Grandma, Michael? She was out shopping with her friends, Helen and Mary, but she's back. I can get her."

"That's okay, Grandpa. Just tell her I send my love. I wish we were going to see you at Christmas, but Mom and Dad said they're staying up North this year, and I can't afford to make the trip on my own."

"Where are you now?"

"At my apartment in Baltimore."

"Well, if it's not too much problem, could you head down to your office and make sure that shipment of oak gets out before Friday? We've got a big order of desks from the Pentagon that can't start until the oak gets here."

I'm growing more agitated with Calvin and his people

at the lumber supplier. They were late with last week's shipment of cherry. Didn't even bother to call with a heads-up.

You just can't find good help anymore... Someone just poked their head into the room and asked if I wanted to help string garland. I don't know who she is, so I tell her to leave me alone.

IT'S FOGGY OUTSIDE.

No, it's not. I'm inside. Lying on a bed. The TV is on. I Love Lucy, but the sound is turned down. The picture comes and goes. The antenna needs to be adjusted, but I can't reach it. There's somebody with me. They have their back to me and they're talking on the phone. They're trying to keep their voice down, but my hearing is perfect.

"He's had two visitors this week. And your son called earlier today... a gentleman named Grady Longacre was here a couple days ago. He comes by every couple weeks... yes, ma'am, from work... your father occasionally knows who he is, but not often... and Claire Tatum, I think she's a family friend, she's been in several times this month and... no, Mrs. Mott, she just signed in as a friend... oh, really? He..."

Claire Tatum?

Claire Tatum!

Oh, my goodness. Does Rosalie know?

"...we could prohibit her from seeing your father, Mrs. Mott, but he receives so few visitors that it might be more beneficial for him to... yes, ma'am, I understand, but you said it was fifteen years ago. The staff has said that he didn't know who she was, so that's... yes, ma'am. I'll do that."

Rosalie is in Baltimore, at Stephanie's house. She can insist that she's there to see Stephanie, Randy, and little Michael, but I know the truth. It's all about Michael. He's seven years old and perfect in every way. Rosie thinks he needs more attention than Stephanie gives him. Stephanie's always at work, it seems. Randy doesn't work enough. I'm glad Rosie has started going to see them again. She refused to leave me at home alone in the first few months after... Claire and me. But Rosalie has to see Michael.

And me and Claire? Since Archie threw her out, she's never in the neighborhood anymore. She called me a couple times at work, but I told her that I can't divorce Rosie. We've been together so long, and a divorce would cost so damned much that...

Claire's ex was an abusive prick named Archie. They lived across the street. Claire didn't socialize with the other women on the street. Archie made sure of that. He'd beaten their three kids for the smallest infractions, and when they were gone, he'd started in on Claire.

"... yes, Mrs. Mott. The doctor seems to think that his condition is worsening..."

She was so helpless, Claire was.

"Deeper into Stage Six, maybe even Stage Seven."

It, Claire and me, started after she backed into our mailbox. It didn't hurt her Oldsmobile, but our mailbox was crushed. She was devastated. I heard her wailing in our front yard and went out. Archie was out of town.

"Was his wife's name Rosalie? He asks about her several times a day... yes, ma'am, he sometimes mistakes other residents for her. We showed him the obituary, but..."

Obituary?
Whose obituary?

"We hope we can help him understand that Rosalie has been gone for two years."

Rosalie?

Gone?

"That's why we feel that Claire Tatum's visits have been beneficial to him... yes, ma'am, I understand. That's your prerogative. I'll see that it gets done."

Claire Tatum?

Claire? Rosalie?

Rosalie Tatum? No, that's not right.

Claire Flanagan? That's what I used to dream. Claire and me married. To each other.

But there was always Rosie.

But, Claire... oh, Claire.

CHAPTER FOUR

"We lost the Sifford Inn account, Neal. I wish I could've done something. I know how much that account means to you, but after all the others left I was..."

His voice is deep and irritating. He says he worked for me, but I don't remember anyone named Grady Longacre. I don't think he's telling the truth.

"Clark Sifford and I have a handshake deal," I say. "Desks, chairs. Boy, are those chairs beautiful. Clark wants the Sifford S carved into the back of every one of them. I told him, 'Clark, that'll add sixty bucks to the cost of each chair,' but he doesn't care."

"Yeah, Neal, I remember. Unfortunately, Clark passed on a few years back, but he hadn't been involved in the hotel's decision-making since they went public. Sad, too, because—"

"Now I know you're lying! Get out of here. I just spoke to Clark Sifford last week. He placed an order for twenty-three new lobby chairs and an extension to their registration desk. I knew you were a phony!"

The guy who calls himself Grady something-or-other gets

a pained look on his face, but I'm not falling for that. I've seen his type before. Scammers who try to weasel their way into your business, then take everything. The same thing happened to Parker Benedetto not more than six months ago. A couple of men came to see him, friends of President Reagan, they claimed. They even had photographs of themselves with the President. And references, too. Parker even spoke on the phone to someone who claimed to be Henry Kissinger before allowing them to invest in his operation. By the time the Feds got involved, there was nothing left. Parker stopped coming to Rotary and withdrew from our circle of friends. When I spotted him in Frawley's IGA three, maybe four, days ago, he ducked down the pet food aisle to avoid me. Sad.

"It makes me sad to see you this way, Neal, but you appear to be in good physical shape. Are you still walking every day?"

"Not like I used to. Between the extra orders at the factory and going to Stephanie's school activities, I barely have time to think."

He nods, then gets to his feet. "You've still got the strong hands and arms of the furniture builder you were when we met. If only we could get the rest of you back. Trevor Stanley has torn apart everything that you—"

"I don't know who you are, but I want you out of here now!" I scramble to my feet and approach him with the intent to toss him out on his ass. He's bigger than me, but he's also older, probably sixty, fatter, slower. His eyes grow wide.

"I let you get away with speaking badly of my friend Clark Sifford, but Trevor Stanley is as fine a young man as you'll ever meet. Now, get the hell out of here before I do something I regret."

He backs out the door, never taking his eyes off me.

"I'm sorry to upset you, friend. You're just not—"

"I'm no friend of yours," I say as I slam the door in his face.

"HE HAD AN OUTBURST THIS MORNING."

"Staff member or visitor? Did it turn physical?"

"Visitor. A man he's known for years. A threat was made, but there was no contact."

They're talking outside the room where I'm staying. I can see them through the partially open door. One is wearing a white coat. He seems to be in charge. The other is the person who brought my lunch. Apparently, they're discussing a problem with one of the people staying here.

"Kevin takes him out to walk on the track most days. He said that several times over the past couple weeks, he's thought that cracks in the sidewalk were large holes. He became fearful and didn't want to continue."

"Those are bad signs," the man in the white coat says. "And indicative of a progression of the dementia. Does he recognize family members?"

"None have been here in months. The daughter lives in Baltimore. She and her husband have a son who just graduated college, but that's it."

"She was the one who complained about the female visitor?"

"Yes. Apparently, he had an affair with her years ago. It broke up her marriage and nearly cost him his."

"Still, she's someone he knows. I can understand the daughter's concern, but she needs to make more of an effort to see him. He needs to have contact with people from his past. What was the woman's name again?"

"Who, Doctor? The daughter?"

"No, the... *other woman.*"

Both of them laugh.

"Her name is Claire Tatum. She's a nice lady, mid-sixties, maybe. About his age."

Claire Tatum.

Claire Tatum?

Are they talking about Claire from across the street?

I raise up and look across the street to see if she's home, but the shade is drawn.

THERE ARE *things that need fixing.*

I sit up in bed and look at the clock. Nine-twenty. Dark, so it must be night.

"Where am I?" I call out. "What is this place?"

There are things that need fixing.

I get up and look around for my tools. Fixing things has always been something that I'm good at. I fixed Stephanie's bicycle after she left it on the street and a trash truck ran it over. It listed a bit but was good as new otherwise.

And the washing machine, the Speed Queen. We've gotten nineteen years out of it because I keep it maintained. Still, Rosalie wants a new one. I'll hold her off as long as I can, but sooner or later, she'll get what she wants. She always does.

There are things that need fixing.

"What are they?" The sound of my voice startles me. The floor is cool under my feet. I need my shoes. Where are my shoes?

I turn around to find them, stumble, and go down hard. My head hits the side of the bed and it hurts like hell. I lie there for a few moments, assessing the damage. I'm fine, but already I feel a headache coming on, like the one I got at the factory the other week when Buster Shockley accidentally smacked me with a length of oak. That headache passed and this one will, too. I get to my feet just long enough to crawl back into bed. I figure I'll lie here for a few moments, then go find out what things need fixing, but the bed feels really good, so the things that need fixing will just have to wait until tomorrow.

PART TWO

CHAPTER FIVE
SATURDAY, DECEMBER 12

I AWAKEN.

I sit up in bed. It's dark. A digital clock on the wall tells me it's three-seventeen in the morning. It also tells me that the date is Saturday, December 12. It doesn't tell me what year it is.

I reach out to turn on the bedside lamp. It's the banker's lamp from my desk at home, the one with the brown glass shade. Most banker's lamps have green shades, and I had to search high and low for this one. I finally found it at an office supply store in Sarasota.

The lamp is from home, but I'm someplace else. Where? The bed is narrow and has rails. A hospital bed. What am I doing in the hospital? I stretch out my feet until they touch the floor, then I stand up. Physically, I feel pretty good, though I have a headache. Maybe that's what I'm here for. I glance at the bedside table and notice three drawers. I pull open the first and find a toothbrush, dandruff shampoo, and other toiletries. Dandruff shampoo? I've never had dandruff a day in my life.

The second drawer contains socks, underwear, and a

file full of paperwork. I remove the file, sit back on the bed, and open it. On top is an envelope with a Baltimore postmark. It's a Christmas card from Michael, my grandson. He's included a photograph. He's all grown up, but I would recognize those eyes anywhere. They're my eyes. Everyone says so. It's a graduation photo from Georgetown University. I flip it over and find he has written a note:

To Grandpa, with love!

Okay, so I've been here for a while. The last time I remember seeing Michael was his junior year of high school. Rosalie and I went up to watch him play lacrosse. We'd never seen lacrosse before, but I could tell he was very good.

But back to now. How long have I been here and why? I feel panic starting to rise, but know that won't do any good, so I push it away and return to the file. There are a bunch of pink sheets of paper, obviously duplicates of some report. I look closer and see my name. Each sheet is labeled *Patient Progress Report*. They're from a place called Pinehurst Pavilion. I glance around the room and spot that same name on a Styrofoam water pitcher. The pink pages are dated, and in reverse order with the most recent on top. I go to the back of the stack and begin reading.

Neal Flanagan is a sixty-six-year-old male who is suffering from middle-stage dementia. He was admitted this week following the death of his wife.

Rosalie is dead.

I'm surprised, but then I'm not. Something deep inside me already seemed to perceive that Rosie was gone. I sit for a moment and grapple with this.

How did she die?

I have no idea. Her heart gave her trouble at times. Was that it?

My last memory is of us sitting on the back porch at home. It was chilly, not even sixty degrees. Our relatives up North would laugh at how we wrapped up in our heavy coats when temperatures got into the fifties, but it's all what you're used to. Anyway, Rosie made soup. Tomato soup. I don't really like tomato soup, but I didn't complain. We ate soup and talked about our upcoming trip to Baltimore to see Stephanie, Randy, and Michael. Michael was starring in his class's holiday production.

Did we go?

I don't remember.

It must be the dementia. The form I'm holding says I'm in the middle stages. How can that be? My mind doesn't feel foggy or anything, but then again, if it did, would I even know?

Rosalie is dead.

And that makes me feel, how?

Sad? Yeah, a little, but there's something between me and my feelings, like a wall that seals off the pain. Rosie and I were together for a long time, more than forty years. The feelings were there at the beginning. But the important ones? The ones that make a person hurt to their very core when something bad happens? Those aren't there. I know why they're gone. It was me. I caused them to go away when I... and Claire. Rosie never really got over that. Things went back to normal, sort of, but something was different after she found out about Claire. We were together, but not really.

I return to the stack of forms. There was a period of time they've documented, about three weeks, when I became belligerent. I refused to eat, swore at an orderly, and knocked my dinner to the floor. I've also been walking a lot, up to four miles a day, on a track at the

Pinehurst Pavilion grounds. That explains why my legs feel great.

The more I read, the more it becomes apparent that my dementia has been getting worse. Two days ago, I approached a female patient, held her hand, and called her Rosalie. The next day I became verbally and physically aggressive with a guest. Grady Longacre.

Grady Longacre?

The ridiculousness of this makes me want to laugh, but I don't because I don't want someone to hear me and come checking. Grady is one of my oldest and dearest friends. I hired him as bookkeeper for the furniture plant two years after I opened the doors, when it became evident that I was better at building and selling furniture than I was at keeping the books. My best friends, Hal Ricks and Vince Garber, said I was crazy to hire a colored man to keep track of my money. I hired Grady as my bookkeeper and found new best friends.

Me attacking Grady is absurd.

But here it is, in black and white.

Patient angrily slammed door in face of visitor named Grady Longacre. No injury.

And then, the top sheet, the most recent.

Patient's daughter has advised staff that Claire Tatum, an occasional visitor, is no longer permitted to see patient.

Claire has been coming to see me.

And I have no recollection of it.

Again, I put my mind to work. The last time I spoke to Claire was when she called the office. It was three weeks after Archie kicked her out, which was two days after he found out about us. Betsy, my secretary who had deduced everything, including my relationship with Claire, had grumbled when she put her call through. I wanted very much to talk to Claire that day, to tell her how sorry I was. It seemed unfair that Rosalie and I had decided to save our marriage while Claire was being kicked to the curb.

But as I stared at the blinking light on my desk phone, I wondered to myself, unfair to who?

What if Rosie had demanded a divorce? Taken half of everything? Forced me to liquidate retirement accounts and investments?

I would still have Claire.

And the six weeks with Claire had been the best of my life.

My hand was shaking as I reached for the phone.

"Claire?"

She was sobbing so hard that she was unable to speak at first.

"I... Archie..."

I could hear her deep breaths as she tried to get control. It didn't matter. I knew what she wanted to say. Archie had already told Rosalie everything, smug in the fact that he'd taught his soon-to-be ex-wife a lesson about infidelity. Rosalie didn't like Archie any more than I did, but they'd formed an alliance of sorts since he'd discovered the emails. I knew that Claire had moved into a tiny apartment over a dry cleaner's shop in Palmetto, getting by on whatever crumbs Archie chose to throw her way.

I'd wanted to tell her that she needed to hire a good attorney, that Florida was a no-fault divorce state, and that she was entitled to part of their marital property regardless of our relationship. It wouldn't work, though. Claire's self-esteem had been next to nothing most of her married life. The difference I'd seen in the six weeks we'd been together was unbelievable. Some people might say it was as if a butterfly had emerged from its cocoon, but those people hadn't seen Claire as I'd seen Claire. It was more like a tiger escaping from the clutches of an abusive master.

But I had promised Rosalie's church-friend-slash-attorney Regina Mankiewicz that I would cease all contact with Claire. Regina had me by the short hairs, and she knew it. If I so much as stepped out of line, Regina would make sure that Flanagan Furniture was a distant memory. She could do it, I suspected. So, as much as it killed me, I promised.

Claire was still crying, still trying to compose herself, when I said with all the authority I could muster four sentences that I didn't mean. "I cannot talk to you anymore, Claire. I want my marriage to work. We should never have done what we did, but it's over and that's that. Don't call me anymore."

And she hadn't.

Later that night, after Rosalie was asleep, I'd crept downstairs, locked myself in the bathroom, and for the first time in my adult life, I cried.

All the promises in the world couldn't make up for the fact that I loved Claire Tatum like I'd never loved any woman, including Rosalie.

And three months after that telephone call, I felt the same.

Six months later, the same.

And a year. And two.

And according to the paperwork I was holding in my hand, that was about the time the dementia started to take over.

But it's not taking over now, is it?

And as I sit here, looking through the stack of reports, diagnoses, and updates, I know just as certain as I know my own name that I still love Claire Tatum.

And that I'm going to find her and let her know.

I check the wall clock again.

It's four-eleven. Still Saturday. Still December 12.

It's dark outside. I want to get up from the bed and flee this place called Pinehurst Pavilion. How hard can it be? Can I just walk away? I rise and check out a closet at the foot of my bed. There are several shirts in my size that I don't recognize. I remove the pajamas I'm wearing and put on one of the shirts. Three pairs of sweatpants and a single pair of khaki slacks are hanging next to the shirts. Who hangs up sweatpants? I pull out the slacks, Dockers, thirty-four waist, and pull them on. Thirty-four is my size, but they are large around the waist. I search high and low, but can't find a belt, so I decide to go without. I pull a pair of white socks from the drawer next to the bed and snicker as I put them on. Dockers and white socks. Who the hell dresses like that? I do, at least today. The only shoes are slippers and a pair of well-worn New Balance sneakers. I choose the sneakers. The pants are way too big and keep drooping to show my Fruit-of-the-Looms, so I return them to the closet and take a pair of the sweatpants that have a drawstring. Grey sweatpants, light-yellow button-down shirt, white socks, New Balance sneakers. I look like I'm escaping from a nuthouse.

It'll have to do.

I step into the tiny restroom that adjoins the room I'm in but don't turn on the light. I pee, poop, wash my hands, pee again, then wash my hands again. In the darkness I'm able to make out a mirror over the sink. Curiosity gets the best of me, and I check to make sure the coast is clear before closing the bathroom door and turning on the light. It takes a few moments for my eyes to adjust to the harsh brightness, and when they do, I wish they hadn't. I'm a mess. A real train wreck. My hairline has receded a couple inches, my hair is totally gray rather than the salt-and-pepper I'm used to seeing. My neck is fleshy and sagging, and there are bags under my eyes that weren't there before. If there were any doubt about the legitimacy of the paperwork I've just read, one look at my face eliminates it. At least I'm tan, probably from all the walking I'm alleged to have been doing.

I return to the bedside table in search of money. I have no idea where Pinehurst Pavilion is in relation to home, so some money for a cab or bus may be necessary.

Nothing.

I'm about to give up when I spy a folded piece of paper in the bottom of a drawer. I examine it closer.

Resident Leave Form.

This could be useful. I fold it back up, put it in my pocket, and return to the bathroom to check myself in the mirror one more time. I could use a shave, but there's no razor, so that'll have to wait. I open the door and step into a dimly-lit hallway with rails on both walls. It looks like every hospital I've ever visited, except for the Christmas decorations, garland and ornaments that hang from the ceilings. And Christmas stockings made from construction paper, like some third-grade art project. One with my name is hanging nearby.

There's a stale smell in the air, an old-person smell. The hall extends just a few doors to my left before dead-ending at a large window. I turn right and start walking. Ahead, I see brighter light. Twenty doors ahead, I come to a nurses' station. I pause to let my eyes adapt. When they do, I see one person, a young man, seated at the station. He's staring intently at his computer screen. I am considering my options when he looks up and spots me.

"Hey, Neal," he says as he points to several chairs across

from the desk. "Pull up a seat. Hey, I meant to tell you yesterday, I looked up Nate Thurmond."

I'm not sure how to respond. If I say too much, will he figure out that I'm thinking clearly? Could that jeopardize my chances of leaving here or make it easier? I look at him quizzically, but don't say anything, despite the fact that Nate Thurmond was my favorite NBA player back in the day.

"Eleven years in the league. Warriors, Bulls, Cavs." The guy appears pleased with himself. "Averaged fifteen a game for some pretty good teams."

He's right on all counts.

"He's no LeBron, but he wasn't a slouch, either."

I have no idea who LeBron is, so I let it go.

"I'm watching last night's Bucks – Clippers game, so if you know who won, keep it to yourself." He smirks as he says this. I get it. He thinks I have no idea who I am or where I'm at. That's okay, though. It's better that he under-estimate me.

I sit quietly for a few moments, maintaining my best poker face as I take in everything. The desk where he's seated is surrounded by labeled files. Two of them catch my eye. Written in large block letters, I see *Resident Leave Forms – Approved* on one of the files, and *Resident Leave Forms – Pending* on the other.

I continue to sit, hopeful he'll have to vacate the desk to pee before I have to again. He must have the bladder of a statue, because forty minutes pass without a word. He studies his computer and occasionally looks at a bank of monitors to his left.

Then, a female nurse approaches, nods at me absently, and goes behind the desk. She lowers her head and whispers to the young man who has concealed his computer screen from her view.

"Seropian in one-fifty-eight has shit himself again."

The young man takes a deep breath and rises. He appears sheepish.

"You were supposed to check him at midnight and three, Harley. But you didn't, did you?"

Her accusation hits home, and the young man, Harley, hangs his head. Seeing she's hit her target, the nurse continues.

"I'm not doing all the work by myself just so you can watch basketball. Now get down there and clean the old man up." The nurse doesn't seem to care that I'm hearing everything she says. She's pissed at Harley and has had enough.

"Will you at least help me turn him over?" Harley's tone is pleading, and I expect her to turn him down cold, but she doesn't. Instead, she looks at me.

"Will he be okay, or should we take him back to his room?"

Harley waves his hand dismissively. "He'll be fine. Probably be asleep in three minutes."

SOMEONE SOMEPLACE CAN PROBABLY SEE me on the TV cameras that feed the screens at the desk. I can see myself on one of them, as I lean over the desk and look around for a moment before reaching for the *Resident Leave Forms – Approved* file and placing it under my shirt. I consider filling it out on the spot but realize I'll be a sitting duck if Harley or the nurse return. Instead, I go back to the room where I've been staying. I'm almost there when I realize I don't have a pen, so I return to the desk for that.

Back in the room, I pee first, then open the file and examine a couple of completed forms. One individual, a Sarah Rideout, has approved both. Her handwriting is neat and easy to read. The rest of the forms have been completed in varying handwriting styles and scrawls. I retrieve the blank from my pocket and get to work. Pretty basic stuff, really. Name of resident, age, gender. I blow through that in a manner of minutes. Then I get to the name and relationship of the person who is signing me out. The small print states that the individual must be a direct relative or friend who has been approved by a relative. Either way, they must be over twenty-one. I choose Stephanie Flanagan-Mott, my daughter. Next is address. *Someplace in Baltimore* probably won't get the job done, so I make up an address. There must be an Oak Street in Baltimore, right?

And just like that, the form is done. I take my time and come up with a pretty good forgery of Sarah Rideout's signature of approval, then place it in the file and check the clock. Five past five.

When I return to the nurses' station, Harley is back watching basketball. He nods but doesn't say anything. I suspect his earlier cheer has been diluted by having to wipe Seropian's ass in one-fifty-eight. I take a seat and wait for the next interruption of his overnight waste of time. It comes at five-thirty, when the kitchen crew begins to straggle in. The front door buzzes as each tries to gain access, and each time, Harley takes a deep breath like it's beyond his physical strength to reach over and push the button that unlocks the door. After seven sets of buzzing, Harley's deep breaths, and the door being opened and shut, I am certain that getting out of here will be easy-peasy. Ten minutes later, the buzzing is over. The kitchen staff has headed to work, and Harley is back watching basketball.

Then, a different buzzer sounds. Harley turns to his left, examines a bank of lights, and pushes one.

"Mrs. Conroy, did you need something?"

The response comes through a tinny speaker. "I've dropped my teeth."

"Can you get up and find them, Mrs. Conroy? We are pretty busy right now." Harley is starting to become more irritated at the morning's interruptions.

"I tried to stand, but felt my legs going out from under me, so I'm back in bed."

Mrs. Conroy is going to be my ticket to freedom.

"I'll be right there." Harley stands, stretches, yawns, and shuffles past.

"Sometimes I wish we could trade places," he says gruffly to me.

And then, he's gone. I approach the desk, place my approved leave form in the file with the others, and push the button that opens the doors.

And I'm gone, too.

It's CHRISTMAS TIME. Santa, snow, and all that.

But this is Florida, so there's no snow. Bradenton has only had one snowfall in recorded history, a few flurries one day back in the seventies. No white Christmas here. As I exit through the front doors of Pinehurst Pavilion, the early morning air is thick with humidity. It's still dark, and the street I'm standing on is narrow and empty. I don't recognize anything, so I start walking west. If you live in

Bradenton and start walking west, you'll always come to water sooner or later. Sarasota Bay or the Gulf of Mexico.

As I approach a crossroad, a car approaches and slows. I can barely make out the driver, a woman who is checking me out before proceeding. Does she work at Pinehurst Pavilion? If so, did she recognize me? What if she goes in and mentions seeing old Neal Flanagan up the block? What would happen? Would they look in the *Resident Leave Form – Approved* file and see that I'd been checked out by my daughter? And if they did, wouldn't it seem strange that I was walking alone just a few blocks away? I pick up the pace until I reach the cross street. The name isn't familiar, so I continue on. Three blocks later I still haven't found a street name I know, and I'm starting to worry that maybe I'm not in Bradenton after all.

Then, I find myself.

Manatee Avenue.

A major east-west boulevard that dead-ends into the Gulf of Mexico at Manatee Beach, a favorite weekend spot for Rosalie, Stephanie, and me, along with a few thousand tourists. I sense the beach calling my name but know that I can't go there now. I have to get home, and home is south and east about thirty blocks. I start walking.

The feelings that come over me as I walk are extraordinary. According to the paperwork in my night-stand back at Pinehurst Pavilion, I was there for two years. Before that, the documentation said that I'd been at home, where Rosalie provided my care. I'm not sure how much time has passed since I walked these streets with a clear mind, but things have changed. The Shake Pit, Stephanie's favorite ice cream stand, has a new sign. Danielson's Appliance Mart is a tattoo parlor. As I walk, several people jog past with earbuds, undoubtedly listening to music. That's not new, but the fact that I don't recognize any of them is unsettling. Then I have a thought that unsettles me even more.

What if home isn't home anymore?

That could be. Rosalie died two years ago. Stephanie might've sold the house. It would make sense. I mean, why keep a house nobody lives in? My stomach starts to knot up as I walk. The sky is lighting up to the east and Manatee Avenue is growing increasingly congested. The smells of gas and diesel fumes assault my senses, so I veer to the south and pick up a parallel street. Quiet again.

Where will I go if the old house is somebody else's? There's always Grady Longacre, but how would he feel about receiving a visit from the ex-boss who'd threatened to kick his ass just a few days earlier?

Claire?

She'd visited, but I had no idea how much her life might've changed. Is she remarried? I've already gotten her tossed out of one marriage. No, I can't risk it.

Forty-five minutes later, I come to the corner of Twenty-ninth and Acevedo. It's an area I know like the back of my hand. Two more blocks and I arrive at Dolphin Court. Home is 617 Dolphin Court. It's an easy address to remember for everyone except the people at the post office who constantly send our mail to 617 Dolphin Drive and vice-versa. Over the years, I became good friends with Lance Shapiro, the taxidermist who lives in a trailer at 617 Dolphin Drive. Because I'd received so many of his holiday and birthday cards, I even know the names of his out-of-state friends and family.

Dolphin Court is a quiet dead-end street at the end of Twenty-Ninth. From a hundred yards away, I spot the familiar oak trees that frame the head of the street. Three houses down I see the pale blue of 617.

Home.

Or is it?

I prepare myself just in case I run into a neighbor who might know of my condition, but there's nobody out. Bruce Marlow's kitchen light is on, but I don't see anyone through the window. Just like Bruce and Cathleen to leave the light on in an empty room. A few steps later and I am standing in front of home. The shades are drawn, but things appear tidy and kept up. The house seems empty, but I can't be sure, so I approach the front door, knock, and wait a few moments.

Nobody comes.

I knock again, then ring the doorbell. From inside I hear the familiar strains of *Don't Worry, Be Happy*. Rosalie selected the Bobby McFerrin tune when I replaced the old doorbell back in eighty-nine. The other selections were John Mellancamp's *Jack and Diane*, Springsteen's *Dancing in the Dark*, and God's *Amazing Grace*. I'd considered replacing it with something more timely or traditional, especially after the thing with Claire and me, but never got around to it.

After several minutes of waiting around, I walk to the corner of the porch, tilt up the concrete flowerpot, and look for the house key.

Not there.

Okay, then. What to do now?

I make my way down the side of the house, trying a couple windows along the way. All locked. Everything looks about the same around back. The pool is clean and inviting. Someone's been cutting the grass, but the shades are drawn here, too. I'm starting to feel like a burglar at my own house as I try the back door. Locked of course. I contemplate putting an elbow through one of the small panes of glass in the door, then I remember the other key.

I kept it in the detached garage, hanging on a hook over my workbench. When I enter the garage, I'm delighted to find my 1997 Buick Riviera parked right where I left it. Despite an accumulation of dust, I'm as thrilled to see it as I would be any old friend. I open the driver side door and inhale deeply, detecting in the scents of English Leather cologne and peppermint candy. I run my hand across the soft leather seat and grip the steering wheel. It's all so familiar, and familiar makes me happy. I'm even happier when I look through the windshield and spot the spare house key hanging on my workbench, exactly where I hoped it would be. Two minutes later I'm walking through the back door of my house, just as I did every day for nearly forty years.

Does it feel strange? Not really. Actually, it feels like any other day. The kitchen is musty from being closed up, and smells of air freshener and, more faintly, of baking. I have to remind myself that it's been at least two years since I've been here, and maybe more than that since I was aware enough of my surroundings to realize where I was. I concentrate, trying to remember the last meal I ate at the painted wood table, but it's impossible. Every meal is like every other meal, an endless parade of pot roasts, spaghetti, and Rosalie's delicious meatloaf. Eating dinner at the kitchen table is just as natural as breathing. Nothing comes through that might trigger a memory of the time I was supposed to be suffering from dementia. I start to wonder if I really had it at all. Maybe the papers in the nightstand at Pinehurst Pavilion were for someone else. Maybe it was all a dream. Maybe Rosie is cleaning upstairs or is at Frawley's IGA getting ground beef and green peppers to make meatloaf.

Her car isn't in the driveway, so that's probably it. She's at Frawley's.

Boy, do I feel better. It was just a dream. Or maybe a bad reaction to some medicine. Whatever it was, it's over now, and I'm not going to say anything about it. Rosalie will think I'm nuts. I go to the pantry in search of a banana or cookie, something to tide me over until Rosalie gets home from Frawley's, but other than three cans of green beans and a jar of pickled beets, the pantry is empty. I glance around the kitchen and notice for the first time how clean it is. Spotlessly clean. Not that Rosie didn't keep a clean house, but this is a different level, like no one is living here. I open the fridge. A half-used bottle of Hunt's catsup, some pickle relish, and more beets. I hate beets.

"Rosie?" I call out.

There's no answer.

I wander from the kitchen into the dining room that we never use. Everything is the same. Same table and chairs, same light fixture, with one bulb burned out. I look toward the living room. The furniture is the same. Leather, tan, bought from Miller's Furniture at their Labor Day sale. Good stuff, not that cheap pleather crap they sell at Furniture Kingdom. There's a TV in the corner, but not the old Magnavox console. This one is bigger and flatter.

And next to the front door, on the table where we used to leave our car keys, there's a folder with a fancy insignia on it. I move closer and pick it up.

Sun State Vacation Rentals

Inside is a typewritten note, dated December 28.

Welcome, Meyerhoff Family from Drexel Hill, Pennsylvania! We hope you enjoy your stay in Gulf Coast Gables, our family home.

Gulf Coast Gables? What the hell?

Gulf Coast Gables was built in 1935. My parents, Neal and Rosalie Flanagan, bought the home from the original owners in 1979. I (Stephanie) grew up in this house and have many wonderful memories here.

Sadly, my father has suffered from dementia since 2012, and has been in an extended-care facility since Mom's death two years ago.

Oh, my goodness.

It wasn't a dream.

Rosie's gone.

My husband, Randy, and I honor them by opening their home to guests like you. We only ask that you enjoy your stay and respect the home and neighbors. Best wishes, Stephanie Flanagan-Mott.

I'VE REREAD the note several times, trying to piece together the puzzle that my mind allowed to scramble.

Rosie is indeed gone. I don't know the exact date, other than it was a couple years ago.

The relationship between Claire and me ended on October 28, 2010. That date I remember. Vividly. I also remember the heartache and hurt I caused Rosalie. She'd done nothing to deserve the pain. She'd remained the same Rosie I married in 1976.

But that was the problem.

People change.

I changed.

As the furniture company grew and became more well-known, I spent more time on the road. I was introduced to and later became friends with United States senators and representatives, with governors and business leaders from around the country. They liked our furniture. They liked its appearance and quality. They liked that we dealt fairly and never cut corners.

They liked me.

I'd started getting invitations. Fishing in Washington State, hunting in North Dakota, crabbing in Maryland. A Congressman from Louisiana took me to the Super Bowl, 49ers and Broncos. I was introduced to famous and powerful friends, and they bought our furniture, too.

I always promised myself that I wouldn't allow those famous connections to change me, but they did. Almost without realizing it, I'd become more cultured and urbane. I'd taken to wearing seersucker suits when I had business outside the plant. Whites, light-blues, and tans. I burnished an image that I thought was good for business. Grady would sometimes tease me by calling me the Colonel Sanders of furniture.

I changed.

Rosalie didn't change.

She remained... Rosalie.

But Claire? Claire was different.

Claire understood the other world, the one I found myself traveling in more and more. She'd been raised by an affluent South Georgia family who'd made their living in candy. The fact that she'd married Arch Tatum a week after college graduation might have removed Claire from her cultured past, but it did nothing to remove the culture from Claire. She'd confided during one of our times together that she'd known straight away that she'd made a mistake marrying Arch. But there was little she could do about it. Her Daddy had provided seed money for Archie to get started in business. That's all he'd needed, it had turned out, as Archie had a real nose for making money.

And for sheltering it from his wife.

So, when that miserable Arch Tatum discovered that his beautiful and perfect wife was having an affair with the guy across the street, he'd cut her out of his life as decisively as one might excise a cancer. And while I felt bad about hurting Rosalie, I'd been devastated by the hurt I caused to Claire.

Because it was Claire who I loved.

ACCORDING to the information in the Sun State Vacation Rentals file, the *Meyerhoff family from Drexel Hill, Pennsylvania* isn't scheduled to arrive at my house, which now is known by the ridiculous title of *Gulf Coast Gables*, until the twenty-eighth of December. Two weeks away. Also included in the folder are phone numbers for area churches, tourist traps, and grocery stores. Since my soul is probably as saved as its going to be, and the last thing I feel like doing is playing mini-golf, I focus on the grocery stores. Frawley's IGA isn't among them, but that's just as well, because Chuck Frawley and his family probably know I'm supposed to be at Pinehurst Pavilion, given how Rosalie and I have shopped there forever.

So, I decide to call a Publix on Manatee Avenue. According to the list, they deliver groceries. I'm happy to find that the wall phone in the kitchen still works. I call the number and someone answers.

"I'd like to have groceries delivered, please."

"Of course, sir, what would you like?"

I hadn't considered this.

"Hmm, how about you just pick some things and bring

them over? I've been away for a while, so I'm pretty much out of everything."

When the girl on the line speaks again, I can tell she thinks I'm nuts.

"Sir, we can't deliver without a list. Maybe you'd like to call back later, when you..."

"Bring me a half-pound of ham, a half-pound of che—"

"What kind of ham, sir?"

"What do you mean, what kind of ham? The kind from pigs. Is there any other?"

The line is quiet for a moment before the girl says, "Sir, we have twenty-nine different varieties of ham. You'll have to be more specific."

This isn't going well. My mind flashes to my Riviera parked in the garage.

"Never mind," I say. "I'll drive over."

BUT FIRST, I need money. I chide myself for my stupidity. Even if the girl had taken my order, how was I going to pay for it?

I have no wallet. No credit cards. No cash.

I begin going through drawers, first in the kitchen, then the living room. Nothing.

I head upstairs to our bedroom. The comforter is new, but the bed is the same. My desk is still in the corner. I used to keep my checkbook in there, along with the MasterCard I never used, so I go to it and pull open the drawers.

Empty.

The closet is empty, too. All my clothes are gone. I'm stuck with the awful outfit I wore to escape.

No money. No clothes.

And damn it, I'm hungry.

THE ATTIC DOOR creaks as I pull it open. It was padlocked, but I used the bolt cutters from the garage to break it open. A dry, hot smell comes at me down the steep steps. Each one groans as I make my way to the top. Light is limited to what little comes from the tiny windows at each end of the attic, so I flip on the light switch at the top of the stairs. Much better.

The space is filled with boxes, some labeled, others not. I pull a couple open and find useless knickknacks. Then, at the back end of the closet, I spot the door to the cedar closet. Rosalie had insisted on a cedar closet. She had furs back then, and furs did better in cedar, she said. I pull open the cedar closet. No furs, but seven of my fine-looking seersucker suits and a variety of shirts, all wrapped in plastic bags emblazoned with the familiar logo of Clipper Cleaners. I'm happy. When I riffle through the pockets, I go from happy to giddy. I always left money in my pockets. Rosalie wanted me to carry a wallet, but seersucker bulges when you put a wallet in the pockets, so I'd taken to carrying a few spare bills. Antoine, the clerk at Clipper Cleaners, was as honest as the day was long. He'd always say, "Mr. Flanagan, you had forty-six dollars in your pants pocket. I kept six for my tip, but the rest of it is still there." What a boy, that Antoine. And sure enough, I find eleven dollars in the pockets of one of the tan suits. The two light blue suits yield twenty-seven and fifty-three bucks. The other four suits are good for a combined one-hundred and eight dollars. A hundred and ninety-nine dollars. On the spot I remove my escape clothes and slip into one of the tan seersuckers, locate a worn but usable pair of socks that I think belonged to Rosalie, and after not finding any of my dress shoes, begrudgingly slip back into the New Balance sneakers.

I can eat.

Life is good.

I TINKER under the Riviera's hood. The note left for the *Meyerhoff Family from Drexel Hill, Pennsylvania* made it clear that the car was off-limits. *Only for family use*, it said. Well, I'm family, and within a few moments, the Riviera is running.

Granted, I probably don't have a valid driver's license. They are only good for eight years in Florida, and I've been out of circulation for at least seven. Even if mine is still current, I don't know where it is. I decide to just take it slow and try not to draw any attention.

Driving is just like riding a bike, I discover. The Riviera has a half-tank of gas and runs pretty well after she gets aired out. Despite her age, twenty-two years to be exact, she isn't as out of place on Manatee Avenue as I might have expected. I'm not either, for that matter. There are plenty of old people driving old cars. It's Florida, after all.

I'm sad to see that Frawley's IGA is no more. The building is empty, the parking lot cracked and overgrown with weeds. To one side of the building, a man with a shopping cart full of belongings is snoozing. I leave him to his rest and head west on Manatee Avenue. A few blocks later, I spot Publix in a shopping center and pull in. There's a thrift store next door, so I run in there. Ten minutes and eighteen dollars later, I walk out with two pair of dress shoes, one white, the other tan, and four pairs of socks. I dump them in the car and head to Publix.

I never cared much for grocery shopping. Rosalie did most of it, leaving me only those quick last-minute trips to pick up things she forgot. The girl on the phone was right. There are lots of types of ham. After contemplating them for a few minutes, I opt for smoked turkey and swiss cheese. I'm searching for bread when I spot a display case full of fried chicken and sub sandwiches. The chicken smells heavenly, so I grab a plastic tub of it. And a sub sandwich. Then I head off for some other stuff.

The bill runs eighty-six dollars and forty cents.

After leaving the market I pull into a K-Mart for underwear. Call me picky, but I just can't bring myself to buy thrift shop underwear. Next door is a liquor store. Ten minutes later I have a six-pack of Hanes and a six-pack of Budweiser. I'm down to seventy-six bucks, but the day is looking better and better.

WHY DIDN'T I leave Rosalie? It was more than the lost stake in the company, wasn't it?

Back home those questions dance through my mind as I enjoy a chicken wing, a turkey-and-swiss sandwich, some coleslaw and a beer.

I planned to, after Claire and I were exposed. Not right away, but within the year. She would be okay. In my well-ordered plan she would move to Baltimore to be close to Stephanie and our grandson, Michael. Stephanie had taken her mother's side. I'd hoped that we wouldn't have to tell Stephanie, but Rosalie said she had no one else to talk to, so she'd confided everything. My relationship with Stephanie had immediately changed for the worse. She was never hostile toward me after that, but always cool and aloof. That hurt. We'd been close when she was growing up, closer than she and Rosalie ever were.

But I'd lost my daughter, that much was obvious. By hurting Rosalie, I'd hurt Stephanie, too. With all that going for me, the question remains, why hadn't I left Rosalie and built a life with Claire?

It was a question without an answer. I was there, at home, then... nothing.

It had to be the dementia. I mean, what else could make my memories hit a brick wall?

And why had the brick wall suddenly been removed?

And then, I have a thought that nearly makes me choke on my beer.

What if the brick wall hasn't been removed?

What if I'm... dead?

Would I even know if I was? Would I be able to differentiate between living and dying?

"God, am I dead?" My voice fills the quiet, startling me.

"Is this what it's like? Am I some kind of spirit, haunting my old home like in the movies?"

I laugh at the possibilities. Will I be able to shake the curtain rods when the *Meyerhoff Family from Drexel Hill, Pennsylvania*, show up in a couple weeks? Wake them from their peaceful slumber and send them fleeing for their car?

It's ridiculous, I know. Would a ghost be able to walk into Publix and buy smoked turkey and fried chicken? Would the liquor store sell a six-pack to a ghost?

The beer.

That's it. It has to be the beer. By now, I've polished off three of them, certainly not too many after a day at the furniture plant, but that's been a few years ago. My dementia years have left me unable to handle my liquor. That's got to be it. And when I stand, I know that to be the case. I sway a bit, nearly stumble, then get my balance. I put away the remaining chicken and the rest of the beers, then peer out the kitchen window into the back yard.

Goodness, the pool looks inviting. The thermometer on the back porch, the same one I put up during the cold snap in eighty-four, says it's ninety degrees. Damn hot for December, but perfect for a swim. Swimming while intoxicated probably isn't a good idea, but the hell with that. I head upstairs for my swimsuit and am pulling open bureau drawers when I remember that all my clothes are either gone or packed away in the attic, so I climb the attic stairs again and start looking around. I have no luck finding a swimsuit, but I do come across the artificial Christmas tree that we bought when Stephanie was twelve. I shove the box holding the tree toward the attic stairs, give it a good push, and let nature take it the rest of the way. After a few minutes of searching I locate three boxes of ornaments. These I carry down myself. I find myself excited to again see our Christmas tree standing in its traditional spot in the living room, but first I want to swim, so I leave the tree and ornaments in the upstairs hallway and head back to the attic in search of a swimsuit.

No luck.

The Hanes tidy-whities will have to do. Fortunately, our backyard is secluded, mostly, from the neighbors' views. Hedges erected by the original owners back in the fifties do their job admirably. Heck, before Stephanie was born, Rosalie and I didn't bother with swimsuits, underwear, or anything. We used to joke that Stephanie might have been conceived on one of the chaise lounges next to the pool. Of course, those trysts always came after dark. According to the clock on the big, flat TV in the living room, it's three-twenty in the afternoon. Night won't come for couple more hours, and I'm ready for a swim now, so I strip out of the seersucker, don a new pair of Hanes, and contemplate another beer before thinking better of it and heading outside. There's a floating raft in the garage, yellow like a banana. I get it out, toss it in the pool, and ease myself into the deep end.

Glorious!

Magnificent!

My arms and legs are stiff, so I swim a couple laps to loosen them up. Then I pull myself onto the banana raft and relax into its softness. It's not fully inflated but has enough air to keep me afloat. My mind starts to drift to past summers. To the laughter of little girls as Stephanie and her friends cavort on Saturday afternoons while I watch from the pool's edge.

Then I think of Claire. We never swam here together, but I can still dream. A man is never too old to dream. Shoot, I was fifty-seven when Claire and I began our relationship. She was fifty-eight. Who begins extramarital affairs at that age?

And yet, it was life-changing. Not just the sex, though it was otherworldly, too. It was so much more. It was the connection. The way we thought the same things and loved the same things. It was how we wanted the same things from the rest of our lives, and we wanted those things together.

Ha. So much for that.

It was... it was...

I AWAKE... in water.

Water?

I'm in our swimming pool. I guess I dozed off. I'm floating on a yellow raft I've never seen before. It's dark. My head hurts.

"Rosie?"

There's no answer. She must've gone to Frawley's for some ground beef. Spaghetti for supper, maybe.

I'm tired. There's probably time for a nap before supper, so I roll off the raft, swim to the edge of the pool, and pull myself out. I search for a towel, but there is none, so I go inside and up the stairs, trailing puddles of water behind me. Rosalie won't like that.

Where's Stephanie? She never goes to the store with Rosie, so she must be in her room. I stick my head in, but she's not there, so I go to our bathroom, dry off with a bath towel, strip out of my underwear, and lie down on our bed. I think about setting an alarm for thirty minutes from now, but don't do it. Rosalie will wake me up when the spaghetti is ready.

IT's night when I awake. Nine-twenty according to the bedside clock. I instinctively reach to my left to touch Rosalie, but she's not there. Her side of the bed is cold. She's in Baltimore, I decide, spending a few days with Stephanie and Michael. Michael probably has a middle school basketball game. I should've gone, but there's too much going on at work. Grady Longacre says I need to trust him enough to take a few days off now and then. I trust him completely, but it's my name on the door, so I need to be there.

I crawl out of bed and proceed into the hallway in the

direction of the bathroom, and trip and nearly fall over a large box. The only light in the hallway comes from a street-light that filters in, but it's enough to make out the Christmas tree box. Was I supposed to put that up while Rosie is in Baltimore? I guess so, because boxes of orna-ments are stacked next to the attic door. It's just like Rosalie to leave the boxes where I'll trip over them, her subtle reminder of the task at hand.

I pee, then return to our room and search the bureau drawers for my pajamas, but the drawers are empty for some reason, so I pull on the seersucker slacks hanging from the doorknob and muscle the Christmas tree box downstairs to the living room. I start to switch on a lamp, but first take a look across the street.

The porch light at Claire's house is on.

Our signal.

I feel myself getting aroused at the thought of being with her. We worked out this subtle form of communication week before last, after our first and second adventures at a cheap motel on the Tamiami Trail. When the porch light is on, Arch is away from home and I'm free to come over. We've used the system just once so far, a few days ago. I had to lie to Rosie, tell her something pressing had come up at the plant. Though it was after nine, she hadn't raised an eyebrow. I'd jumped into the Riviera and headed up the street and around the corner where I parked the car in the lot at the Jiffy Mart and made my way down the alley behind Claire's house. She was waiting for me. The next two hours were heavenly.

And again tonight, the light is on.

The Christmas tree will have to wait.

I race back upstairs and slip into a white shirt and jacket that matches the seersucker slacks I'm wearing. My heart is racing in anticipation. It's as if I'm seventeen again. I search for shoes but can't find them. My closet, like the dresser, is empty. What the hell has Rosie done with my clothes?

Oh well, I'll go barefoot.

I go back downstairs and hunt for the keys for the Riviera. As I'm looking for them, I glance out the front window again.

The porch light is off.

The opportunity is missed.

My heart sinks.

The Christmas tree will be put up after all.

CHAPTER SIX
SUNDAY, DECEMBER 13

I AWAKEN AND KNOW EXACTLY WHERE I AM.

My neck hurts. I'm on the living room sofa, face-down. The haze that is my brain clears and I remember yesterday.

Pinehurst Pavilion.

My escape.

Walking home.

My seersucker suits in the attic.

Shopping at Publix.

Eating fried chicken and smoked turkey. Drinking beer. Drinking more beer.

Swimming.

A crushing headache.

Then, nothing else.

How did I wind up on the living room sofa?

And the Christmas tree? I left it in the upstairs hallway, yet here it is, out of the box, branches spread about the room, looking as if a tornado struck.

At some point yesterday, clarity gave way to fog. My brain returned to wherever it had been. But now, it's clear again. The fog is gone. That makes me happy.

And hungry.

I did a pretty good job of getting the necessities at Publix yesterday, but forgot to address breakfast. I also forgot to get a razor and shave cream, and I'm pretty scruffy. That might have worked for Don Johnson in the *Miami Vice* days, but everyone in Bradenton knows that Neal Flanagan maintains a clean-cut image, so first on the day's agenda: a shave and breakfast.

IT'S SEVEN-TWENTY. The first two diners I drive to don't exist anymore, but the third, Crager's on Fourteenth Street, is still there. I fold into a breakfast of bacon, eggs, sausage, toast, hash browns, and enough coffee to float a cruise ship.

"Nice suit you got there," the waitress compliments me on my light-blue seersucker. She's about my age, obviously a woman who appreciates style. I leave her an extra generous tip, despite the fact that I'm down to sixty-five dollars.

"Do you know of any barbershops in town where a man can still get a shave?" I ask her.

"Hon, it's Sunday. Barbers don't usually work on Sundays."

Dang it, she's right.

"Sorry, it slipped my mind."

"Tell you what, hon, let me go make a call, and I'll be right back."

My senses were instantly on high alert. Had she figured me out as an escapee from some long-term care unit? Did the old suit give me away? I consider making a dash for it but haven't paid the check yet. I pull out my money and peel off a twenty. I'm just about to leave it on the table when she returns. She hands me a yellow slip of paper.

"Lefty's on Fifty-third, next to the pet store," she answers. "A couple of my lawyer customers go there. He's not open today, but I know he goes in Sunday mornings to catch up on paperwork, so I called him. He says to come on down."

I drive to the area she described. The place is locked, so I rap on the door. A man appears from in back, forties, bearded, and heavily tattooed. Not exactly what I expect from a barber, but it's Sunday, and he's been kind enough to open up. On the way over I've prepared a story that I hope is convincing enough.

"Thanks so much. I've been in the hospital for a while. I just got out yesterday and didn't realize how scruffy I looked until I got home."

Lefty smiles and says it's okay. He points to an old-fashioned barber chair the likes of which I haven't seen since I was a kid.

"Shave and a haircut," I say as I climb into the chair, resisting the urge to add, *six bits*. Lefty gets to work. We talk about life and love and politics, typical barbershop chatter. I leave most of the talking to him, aware that any opinions I espouse are probably outdated. Lefty goes on and on about how Donald Trump is messing up the world. I'm aware of Donald Trump. I know about his hotels, but don't know how he can mess up the entire world. But never argue with a guy holding a razor to your neck, right? Lefty seems to have a real affinity for a person named Obama somebody or other. I want to ask who the guy is and why Lefty likes him so much, but that might give away the fact that I've been locked up. He veers off to how bad the Tampa Bay Buccaneers are this season. That's something that hasn't changed.

I gulp when Lefty tells me the price of my haircut and shave but try to hide my surprise as I hand over the cash.

There is now twenty-two bucks in my seersucker pocket. I consider going home to look through the attic for more cash but decide instead to drive out to the plant. I don't know what I'll do when I get there, but it certainly will be nice to see the place.

I head east on Cortez Road, one of the city's busiest thoroughfares. Bradenton is the same, but different. The storefronts, most of them, are like they always were, but many of the names have changed. And traffic is a bitch. I know the snowbirds are the panacea for our economy, but they drive like shit and clog up the main roads. It takes twenty minutes to get clear of the worst of the traffic, but finally I'm on the road to the plant. It's located in a 1960's era industrial park, and when I pull off the highway, I'm amazed to see a five-story addition on the building's west side. The signage out front, including the logo that I designed myself, is the same, though. I'm humbled to see that Flanagan Furniture has withstood the test of time, and judging by the new addition, prospered.

There's a lone car in the lot, parked on the original east end of the building that I know so well. The car is parked in the same spot that used to belong to Grady Longacre, next to the spot that used to belong to me but is now marked for handicap parking. I consider using it anyway, for old time's sake, but instead pull in a few spots away, get out, and approach the same front entrance I've used thousands of times before. It feels the same as it always did, as if I was just here yesterday. It's obvious, though, that I wasn't. This entrance has been dwarfed by the new addition a hundred feet to my right, which has a clerestory and beautiful landscaping. The old entrance, my entrance, looks like a forlorn afterthought. I approach and peer inside the old section, expecting to see the same two desks from where our receptionists worked, but instead there is emptiness. And a sign.

Please proceed to reception area at front entrance.

"This is the front entrance," I grumble to myself. For old time's sake, I pull at the door. It's locked, of course. As I'm taking one last glimpse through the brown-tinted glass, I see movement. A man, dark of skin and gray of hair.

Grady Longacre.

Our eyes lock, and it's as if he's seen a ghost. Because, maybe in some respects he has. He stands there for a moment, blinking rapidly, probably trying to reconcile what he thought he knew with what is right in front of him, then he approaches and pushes open the door. The first thing I notice is how old he seems. The hair wasn't gray before. The posture not as stooped.

And the eyes. What is it about Grady's eyes?

And as he welcomes me, I know with certainty what I see in Grady Longacre's eyes.

Defeat.

"Neal?" His tone is tentative, his bearing protective, like I might jump at him without warning.

Then I remember the report in my file at Pinehurst Pavilion.

Patient angrily slammed door in face of visitor named Grady Longacre. No injury.

"I come in peace," I say gently, offering my right hand. "I promise not to slam the door in your face this time."

Those few words appear to wash away the guardedness in Grady Longacre's bearing. His face grows soft, his eyes shine with joy.

"I don't know what in the hell is going on," he says in his deep rumbling baritone, "but I'm sure happy to see you!"

And with that, Grady pulls me into an embrace that I

happily return. This man knows me better than any male on earth. Better than any female, too, except Rosalie and maybe Claire. We've weathered many storms together, me and Grady. Cashflow emergencies, late shipments, upset customers. The one constant has been each other.

We unclench after several moments, then Grady takes a step back, glances around, and says, "Get in here before somebody sees you."

THE NEXT NINETY minutes pass like two. I can't explain how I am suddenly better, and Grady can't either. He roars with laughter when I tell of my escape, then grows somber when I explain how I slipped back into the fog last night.

"I don't know how long I have, Grady. Maybe I'll go to sleep tonight and never remember anything, but until then, I'm going to enjoy myself."

We talk. We talk about life since I faded away. His daughter, Hayley, married a wonderful young man from Atlanta six years ago. Rosalie and I went to the wedding. Grady's wife, Violet, died in a car crash four years ago. Rosalie and I went to the funeral. I remember neither event.

Grady tells me about Rosalie's passing from cancer two years before. "You were at your worst by then," he said. "They had to keep you strapped in a wheelchair or you would just flail to get out and try to escape." I was, according to Grady, taken from Rosalie's funeral to Pine-hurst Pavilion. What he doesn't say, but I sense, is that Stephanie wanted nothing to do with me.

"My... relationship with Claire really... Stephanie never forgave me."

Grady nods, but doesn't say anything. He knows about

Claire and me. Everybody knows about us. Claire's husband made sure of it. There's nothing Grady can say. It becomes obvious that a change in subject is necessary, so I make it.

"Why are you at work on Sunday?"

Grady raises his hands as if the answer should be obvious. "I've always liked coming in for a couple hours on Sunday morning. Back when you were in charge it gave me time to catch up on the paperwork you threw my way all week."

I punch his arm playfully, like I used to do when we were younger men. "That's a bunch of hooey and you know it. You were always two steps ahead of me when it came to the paperwork that kept this place afloat."

Grady starts to say something, but pauses, so I charge ahead.

"So, tell me about the factory. I'm impressed to see that new addition. Things must be rolling along quite well."

"How about a tour?" Grady asks. "It might help you understand."

"I'd love to see everything. Are Richie and Draymond still the shop stewards?"

Grady sighs but doesn't answer as he motions for me to follow. We pass the door to my old office. There's a shadow where my nameplate used to be, but the door is devoid of any identification.

"I'll explain after our tour," Grady says, not breaking stride.

Everything else looks pretty much as it did when I used to come in every day. According to Grady, the last day I reported to work was a January day seven years ago. "You were coming in before pretty regularly, but you'd started to slip," he explains. "You would sit at your desk and look at magazines. Sometimes you would stay on the same page for two or three hours. When you went for coffee and didn't return for the third time in a month, Betsy told Rosalie it was time to see a doctor."

Betsy was my secretary, the third most tenured employee of Flanagan Furniture, after Grady and me. Grady tells me that she retired three months after I stopped coming in.

"Trevor must've been devastated," I say, speaking of Trevor Stanley, the young man I'd hired to join our leadership team. Grady arches his eyebrows but says nothing. As we approach the large double doors that separate the office area from the shop, he takes out a single key, inserts it into the lock, and pulls open the door. I expect to be greeted by the familiar smells of sawdust and varnish. If it were a workday, there would also be the sound of power equipment.

Today there is neither.

Grady steps into the dark shop and switches on the overhead lights. Thirty-thousand square feet of shop space, at one time the heart, lungs, and soul of Flanagan Furniture, is mostly empty.

Empty.

I take it all in while my stomach does flip-flops. On the far end I see several pieces of familiar equipment, but only a small percentage of what used to be. They are surrounded by desks, cabinets, and other items that, even from a distance, I recognize as our products.

"Repairs," Grady says quietly. "This is where we fix broken legs and drawers. You asked about Richie and Draymond earlier. Draymond has been gone for five years. Richie still works here, but all he does is make repairs. The union was busted years ago. We haven't made a stick of new furniture here for two years."

I don't know what to say. So much empty space. Usable empty space. Yet Flanagan Furniture still is a thriving entity, or at least it appears that way. I wish that Grady would continue talking, but he's as saddened by what is in front of us as I am.

"I'm responsible for this part of the operation," he finally says. "I arrange for pickup, repair, and delivery of the stuff we used to make. We still honor the lifetime warranties, Neal. Do you want to know what Trevor calls them, though?"

"What?"

"The Neal Flanagan albatross."

I laugh harshly. "What's the deal, Grady? Are you and Trevor at odds?"

"You could say that."

"Why?"

Grady shifts uncomfortably from one leg to another as he stares vacantly across the shop. I'm about to push the issue when he speaks again.

"You weren't in a position to know it at the time, Neal, but the country went through a bad spell a few years ago. A lot of old-line companies like Flanagan Furniture lost everything. We took quite a few big hits, but the worst was our retirement plan."

"You set that plan up yourself, Grady. I remember going through it line-item by line-item with you the night before we bought in."

Grady takes a deep breath. "Almost overnight it lost eighty percent of its value. You and Rosalie had tucked enough money away to weather it..." Grady pauses to take another breath. "But people like me and most of the guys in the shop, we didn't save as prudently as you."

When Grady grows quiet again, I don't push. It's obvious that he needs time, so I give it to him,

"I planned to retire at fifty-five," he says slowly. "I'm sixty now. If it weren't for the agreement I have with Trevor, I'd have to work until I'm eighty.

"Agreement?"

"Confidentiality agreement. I signed it four years ago. I maintain my position with the company, at least on paper. My salary goes up ten percent a year, and when I reach sixty-two, I retire with a full pension, compliments of Flanagan Furniture."

"It sounds like Trevor did you a good turn."

I'm standing behind Grady and off to one side, so I've been unable to see his face. When he finally turns and faces me, his eyes are blazing, and his fists are clenched.

"This place stinks worse than a polecat's asshole, Neal. And Trevor Stanley is at the center of it."

I'm floored. I hired Trevor Stanley when he was a fresh-faced twenty-five-year-old with an MBA from Florida State. Grady enthusiastically agreed with the decision. We'd immediately put him to work on some of our biggest areas of need, most notably technology and distribution. Trevor did himself – and us – proud. We were able to cut costs and turn profits almost immediately, and our customers, many of them high-ranking government agency heads, lauded our technological advancements as heartily as they did our products.

But still, as much of a shooting star as Trevor had proven to be, there was never a plan in place where he leapt over Grady on the barebones Flanagan Furniture organizational chart.

"I've come to your room at Pinehurst Pavilion every week for the past two years," Grady continues. "I've told you everything. Even though you didn't really hear it, I felt better unburdening myself."

"Clark Sifford?" I say, almost without realizing it.

Grady looks at me questioningly.

"You told me once that we'd lost Clark Sifford's business."

"That was a couple weeks ago. You remember?"

I nod. "And you started to say something about Trevor, but..." I stop speaking as a stray memory breaks through the brick wall. Grady sees that I remember. He smiles.

"You wanted to beat the shit out of me."

"I read about that in the reports."

Grady rubs the back of his neck and says, "Can you remember what I said when you came at me that day?"

I can't.

"I said, don't come at me unless you're willing to finish me off."

"Meaning what?"

Grady looks away, doesn't answer. Then it dawns on me what he is implying.

"It's pretty bad, huh, Grady?"

He won't look at me, but I can see he's struggling to maintain his composure. His shoulders start to heave, and he takes a deep choking breath. I step forward and place my hand on his beefy shoulder, a gesture that brings forth still more emotion.

We stand like that for a bit, until Grady regains control. I love this man. I have since soon after I hired him, when I saw how loyal he was to the company and me. The aforementioned brick wall separating my life then from today might have changed many things, but that love is still there. The fact that Grady is hurting also hurts me.

"Enough about work," he says. "For whatever reason,

you're suddenly standing in front of me for the first time in a decade. You're thinking clearly and talking clearly." Grady's eyes twinkle as he takes in my attire. "You're even wearing the same clothes you wore back in the eighties and nineties."

I feel my face grow red. "There's nothing left in the house. I found these in the attic."

"Trust me, friend, it only adds to the specialness of the moment. Hey, how about some lunch?"

It seems like I just finished breakfast, but if Grady wants to go to lunch, I'm in. What he says next eliminates any lingering doubt.

"Star Fish Company has stone crab."

My mouth begins to water. Star Fish down in Cortez used to be my go-to place.

"Is it like before?"

"Same great food. Still eating on the picnic tables in the hot sun."

"Then let's go."

We're headed for the shop exit when Grady pauses. "Meet me at my car, Neal. I have one phone call to make, then I'll be ready."

"Will do." I go through the door first. Grady locks up and goes in the direction of his office. As I watch him retreat, I have a thought.

"Grady?"

He turns.

"Are you calling Pinehurst Pavilion?"

He blinks several times.

"Because if you do, they'll figure out that I jumped the fence and will probably be obligated to come get me."

Grady glances at the floor, then at the wall just over my shoulder, then at me.

"You don't think it's dangerous? I mean, what if you relapse?"

I shrug. "They'll take me back and lock me up, then they'll make sure that I never get out again."

I watch while Grady considers this. I think about pleading, but that would make both of us uncomfortable. Then Grady smiles and I realize the moment has passed.

"I still have a quick call to make, but I won't blow the whistle on you. Give me five minutes."

THE LADY at the counter thinks she recognizes me but isn't sure. It's been a long time.

Grady, however, she knows. She calls him by name when she tells him what he plans to order. Grady nods enthusiastically and tells her to double it. "And another order to go," he adds. Then we find a seat.

Star Fish Company is located on an old fishing pier that is still used to drop off the catch of the day. Two dozen picnic tables, some with umbrellas, others without, are crammed in willy-nilly. We've scored a table with an umbrella, but the Florida sun still beats down. I drink beer, Grady has unsweetened iced tea. Our food arrives in two identical white boxes, and I know what I'm going to find inside before I open it. All these years later the place is predictable. And delicious. Stone crab, fries, and coleslaw served with plastic utensils. Simple, priced right, and as tasty as anything I've ever eaten.

"Pinehurst Pavilion must serve bland food, because the stuff I've eaten since breaking out has been..." I can't think of the words to describe how delectable the food has been. All I can offer is a shake of my head. Grady laughs when I tell him about yesterday's smoked turkey and fried chicken. He laughs harder when I bring up the beer.

"Maybe you're cured," he offers. "Or healed, though my understanding from talking to Stephanie is that there's no cure for dementia. It only gets worse. That's been the case with you, at least until yesterday."

"I should call Stephanie," I say.

"No." There's no doubt from his tone that Grady thinks this is a bad idea. He sees I'm stung by his answer. "She hasn't been to see you in over a year."

"People get busy, Grady." I'm not sure why I feel the need to defend my daughter to my best friend. He shrugs, then starts to say something but stops when the woman who took our order brings by a large plastic bag.

"Here's your to-go order, Mr. Longacre."

"Thank you, Shelley," Grady replies as he flashes a smile. "It was as good as ever."

Shelley beams at his praise, then turns her attention to me. "Excuse me for being so forward, but don't I remember you from a few years back?"

I start to speak, but Grady interrupts. "Long-time friend who is back visiting, Shelley. You have a good memory."

As Shelley departs, I have a thought. "Grady, I didn't pay for my lunch." I reach into my pocket, but Grady shakes his head.

"It's on me, friend. Do you even have any money?"

I tell him about the cash I found in my suits. It cracks him up. "Yeah, you always said a wallet interfered with the lay of your seersuckers, whatever the heck that means. You thought you were quite the pretty boy, didn't you?"

I daintily wipe at the lapel of my jacket. "I'm still quite the pretty boy, Grady. Can't you see that?"

Grady gets to his feet, a movement that I can see pains

him. He picks up the to-go bag and motions for me to follow. "I have to make a quick stop to drop this off for a friend," he says as we walk to his car. The air in his sedan is warm from the sun. That and a full belly give me a sleepy, contented feeling. I wonder if I'm going to lose track of things as the day progresses, like yesterday. Then, I have a thought.

"Why did you tell the server I'm a visiting friend? She remembered me from when we used to come here."

"Bradenton might be teeming with tourists and snow-birds, but it's still a small town at its core. I figure the fewer people who know of your miraculous recovery, the better."

"Why, Grady? As I see it, why not just go with it?"

"Hear me out first," Grady says. "If you feel the same after we've talked more, you can lead the Christmas Parade through downtown as far as I'm concerned."

"Start talking, then."

Grady starts to speak, then reconsiders. He points with his thumb toward the food in the back seat. Let's drop that off first, then maybe later..."

We turn into a working-class area of town. Duplexes line both sides of the street. The cars are mostly older models, dusty and forlorn. Grady pulls up in front of a gray stucco unit, retrieves the to-go bag, and opens his door.

"I'll be just a minute. Come with me. I want you to meet my friend."

I would prefer to stay in the car, but Grady's doing so much for me I feel obligated to follow. The two front doors on the duplex share a common sidewalk. Grady goes to the left and knocks on to sixties-era storm door. We wait a few moments. The sun is hot, and I'm starting to question my choice of clothing.

Then the door opens, and my world turns upside down.

I DIDN'T INTEND *to have an affair.*

Rosalie and I had been married for thirty-four years, and I'd never considered being with another woman.

Not Alicia, the busty young receptionist we hired at the factory, who everyone ooh'ed and ahh'ed over. She'd been very attentive to me, so much so that Grady had started kidding me about it, but I was too busy at work for anything like that. Alicia eventually left to get married.

Not Terri, the buying agent from the Department of Agriculture. Those folks in the Ag Department loved our furniture, and it seemed Terri and I were always talking on the phone. We eventually met in Washington, when I went up to check on some work we'd done. We had dinner. Terri wanted more. She was younger than me, raven-haired and beautiful, but I had a reputation in DC as a good man, and I wasn't about to mess that up.

Don't get me wrong. I've never been what someone would classify as a catch. Flanagan men are slightly-built with unremarkable features. I fit the mold perfectly. I didn't exactly get around in high school. Rosalie was the first and only woman I slept with.

Until Claire Tatum.

Claire and Arch moved to the neighborhood in ninety-one. Arch talked too much about himself, Claire didn't talk much at all. They had three kids; we had Stephanie. She became friends with Ryan Tatum, who was a year older. They dated a few times, but things never progressed past friendship. Still, he told Stephanie things. Like about Arch's temper, and about how he turned that temper against his kids. Stephanie told Rosalie. Rosalie told me. Rosalie and I always hoped it would end when Elizabeth, their youngest, left home. I would find out that it hadn't.

The day that Claire backed over our mailbox she seemed like a scared and wounded bird. The first thing I noticed was how she cowered from me when I pulled open the door of her Oldsmobile. That and how she was crying as if she'd just backed over a person instead of a mailbox, apologizing over and over again.

"I've got a post-hole digger in the garage," I said, trying to sound comforting. "I'll have the box up again in ten minutes."

"But... but..." she blubbered something about how dented the box was, about how she would replace it.

"It was already dented pretty good," I said. "Some boys from the middle school threw a pumpkin at it last Halloween. I've got a new one in the garage but haven't gotten around to putting it up yet. You did me a favor."

I smiled and tried to act all Gomer Pyle-golly-gee so she would calm down. It started to work. What I really wished at the time was that Rosalie was home, but she wasn't, so I moved Claire's car back into her driveway.

"It didn't even leave a scratch," I noted as I handed her the keys. Claire was still shaking as she apologized one more time and disappeared into her house.

That should have been the end of it.

But a half-hour later, as I was replacing the mailbox, she appeared on her front porch.

"Mr. Flanagan, would you like to come over for some lemonade after you're done?"

Usually I would've said no. Arch wasn't home and neither was Rosalie. But the expectant look on her face made my decision for me.

"Yes, Mrs. Tatum, I sure would."

Nothing happened that day. I sat at her kitchen table and drank two glasses of lemonade. We talked. I learned about her past. She stopped short of saying anything about her marriage, but there was something there, just under the surface. After forty-five minutes, I stood up to leave. When I handed her my empty glass, our fingers touched. I felt something and could tell she did, too. She looked into my eyes and thanked me again. This time I sensed she wasn't thanking me for taking care of the mailbox.

Over the next several weeks, our paths crossed more than they had in all the previous years combined. There were little snippets of conversation across the street, waves and smiles when our vehicles passed. I found myself looking forward to those moments.

And then, it happened. Arch was in Cincinnati; Rosalie was at Stephanie's place in Baltimore. I was mowing the lawn when Claire asked if I wanted to join her for dinner.

"Nothing fancy," she said lightly. "Lasagna."

I went.

We talked. We talked more than we ever had before. I was learning how incredibly strong Claire Tatum was. And how much she was dealing with at home. She confided that she was considering leaving but was worried about how Arch might react. She was scared of him, and from what I heard, she had reason to be. At one point she started crying. I comforted her.

We spent the night together.

And the next night.

And the next.

I fell in love.

CLAIRE IS STANDING in the door. She looks almost as she did years before, and just the sight of her takes my breath away.

She is wearing a simple white skirt and sleeveless aqua blouse. She is slender and surprisingly firm for her age, our age, and looks stunning. Her hair is short and gray and perfect. She's wearing makeup and smells wonderful. I can't believe that I'm here. Or that she's here. My mind wants to play tricks on me, but I won't let it. This is too real. And too important. She doesn't seem surprised to see me, which tells me that she was the call Grady had to make before we left the factory. And here we are standing two feet apart, neither making a move to touch the other. Just gazing at one another until she extends her hand. I take it. We go inside. Grady doesn't.

WE MAKE LOVE. Little is said. When I try to talk, she gently places her index finger on my lips and whispers, "If you're a dream I want it to last forever."

When I was younger, in my teens or twenties, I sometimes wondered if old people had sex. Of course, back then, old meant anyone over forty. As Rosalie and I entered our older years, I came to the conclusion that old people did have sex, just not often or with much creativity. My six weeks with Claire had opened the door to passionate love-making as I'd never known. I'm feeling all of those things again, and then some. She's beautiful and sexy and experienced in ways that no twenty-year-old will ever know, and as we reach a crescendo, I think that I could die right now and not feel like I've missed anything this life can offer.

Don't get me wrong, I don't want to die right now, but if I did...

We're spent and sweaty and panting. I notice my surroundings for the first time. The bedroom is small and plain with simple window coverings and furnishings. The bed is a double. Most couples would say they could never sleep in a double, but right now I'm cherishing the proximity to this beautiful and sensuous woman. She reaches up and kisses me on the lips. The feelings I'm having threaten to short-circuit my nervous system, but I don't care. My mind, the bane of my existence for the past decade, is sharp and clear. Colors are vivid, scents are intoxicating. I feel young and virile and strong. We've barely spoken, but our eyes and hands and moans have communicated plenty. I wonder if words will actually pass between us, and if it really matters. Claire decides that it does matter.

"I came to see you," she says softly. "But Stephanie..." Tears form in the corners of her eyes. I reach up and wipe at them with my fingers. "She had forbidden me from coming to see you, but then I heard that Grady was your only visitor, so I..." she takes a breath and continues, "...you looked so healthy when I came, and it made me feel good to be with you. I held your hand and combed your hair. Then, someone from there called me. I was not to visit anymore." She buried her face in my chest. "I thought I'd never see you again, but you came back."

"I don't know for how long, but I'm here." I tell her about the past two days. She hangs on every word, then grows concerned when I explain how my condition went downhill as yesterday wore on.

"I'll take care of you if that happens," she says, kissing me in a way that communicates far more than her concern. I feel a warmth coursing through me that reminds me that older people do indeed still make love. I smile at the naiveite of my youth as I push aside an oncoming headache and give in to the feelings.

IT'S DARK, and I don't know where I am.

It's a place I've never been before, or don't remember.

And then, I know. The small room, almost claustrophobically small.

My college dorm room.

It's exam week, and I haven't studied enough for my Organizational Theory class.

"I need to get up."

A hand from behind me comes to rest on my shoulder. Soft, gentle, caressing. It moves down my arm and pulls me back.

"You can sleep a bit longer, Neal," a woman's voice says. I allow her to pull me back toward her. She is naked. I feel her breasts against my back, soft, warm, and incredibly inviting. I'm naked, too. It all feels so good and comfortable. Then her hand moves down my arm, coming to rest on my hip. She strokes gently. I feel myself responding...

CHAPTER SEVEN
MONDAY, DECEMBER 14

I AWAKEN AND KNOW EXACTLY WHERE I AM.

I smell coffee.

And bacon.

Coffee and bacon, and maybe some other scents, but those pale to coffee and bacon.

I rub the sleep from my eyes. The dreamy haze clears away, and for the third day in a row I know exactly where I am.

And who I'm with.

And what we've done.

And done again.

Damn, I feel fine. My head is clear, and my body feels satiated. The woman I love is someplace close by, brewing coffee and frying bacon. I throw the covers back and start to rise when she sashays in wearing a white bathrobe that provides a vexing peek of cleavage. She smiles, beams really, bends over, and kisses me on the lips while her arms wrap around my naked waist. Her right hand pinches my backside. She sees and feels the effect she is having on me, considers it for a moment, then says, "You need to see Grady today."

"Seeing Grady is not on the list of things I want to do."

She giggles like a schoolgirl. "Come into the kitchen and eat."

She goes to the cramped closet and pulls out a fluffy bathrobe nearly identical to hers except for the Marriott logo on the front. It's likely a leftover from her days with Arch, but I don't care. I slip it on and follow her to the kitchen. She points to the seat at the head of her tiny table, where she's set a plate of steaming food next to a cup of black coffee. As I begin tearing into eggs and hash browns and bacon, she takes a seat and watches me, occasionally stroking my arm and hand. I suspect that she's wondering how much of yesterday I remember, but when she doesn't ask, I volunteer. She nods happily as I recount our afternoon, up to a point where we were dozing after making love.

"How did I do?" I ask between bites.

"You were magnificent," she gushes.

I feel myself blush. "No, what I meant was, how did I do remembering?"

She shrugs. "I could tell when I started to lose you. It was after five, maybe six. We were talking, then you became quiet. We came in here and ate the crab claws Grady left us, but you were pretty much gone by then."

I take her hand. "I'm so sorry."

"No," she says, squeezing my hand. "Don't be. We went back to bed. You were quiet, but... shall we say, responsive to my attention."

This surprises me. "You mean, we...?" I can't stop the grin that spreads across my face.

"Twice more. As I said, you were much quieter, but you still knew what I needed and..." she winks.

I'm still trying to process this when she speaks again. "I want you to stay with me, here, for however long you are able."

"I would like that."

Claire stands and picks up my now empty plate. "But right now, Grady really needs to see you. Something came up that he needs to talk to you about."

"Any idea what?"

Her face conveys concern. "Trevor Stanley knows you were at the factory yesterday."

"And Grady feels we need to be worried about that?"

Claire nods. "Trevor called him late last night after your car showed up on security footage. According to Grady, he was livid about your being there. He told Grady that you are a danger to yourself and others and should be taken back to the nursing home. Grady promised that he would get you back to Pinehurst Pavilion."

This makes my gut clench. "I'm not ready to go back." I start to rise from the table, but Claire waves for me to stop.

"Grady's not taking you back, but he does need your help. I'm not sure what's going on, but I know that Flanagan Furniture has really changed over the years."

I tell Claire what little I gleaned from Grady.

"He checks on me now and then, makes sure I'm okay," she says. Her words cause my defenses to rise. She picks up on it and takes my hand. "There's nothing romantic between us, Neal. There never will be. I'll never know another man like you. That's why I'm trying to spend my time enjoying you instead of questioning what brought you back.

"It might be temporary."

"I know," she replies. "And I'm willing to accept that. What I don't want to do is waste the time we have by being concerned about tomorrow. If it were anyone besides Grady, I would tell them to get lost, but he really needs you."

"Then, I guess I need to get showered and dressed."

"Grady came by late last night and left one of your clean suits. It's hanging in the bedroom closet. He'll be here in forty-five minutes, and if you don't mind, I think I'll join you for that shower."

IT's eight-thirty when Grady knocks at the door. I'm dressed in the white seersucker he dropped off last night. Claire, still in her robe, is behind me when I open the door. Grady looks at me, then at Claire peering out from behind me, and smiles.

"A pleasant evening?"

I want to provide a witty answer but can't think of anything. Then Claire pinches my backside and I start to giggle. A moment later, we're all giggling.

"Claire, I promise to return him safe and sound," Grady says as we take our leave. Back in the car, though, his tone changes.

"Did Claire tell you about Trevor?"

"Yes, and that you promised to return me to Pinehurst Pavilion."

"He thinks you stayed at my house last night. I told him that and lied about taking you back, so he wouldn't send any of his people out to get you. If he were to call Stephanie, I don't know what would happen. Fortunately, Trevor is in

Cambodia for a few days before Christmas, or at least that's where I've been told he is."

"Cambodia? You mean, by Vietnam?"

Grady nods. "He goes to that region often, Neal. That's part of what I want to talk to you about. Let's go back to the factory."

"Do you think it's safe?"

"I want him to know that I brought you by again. He'll call me tonight to check and make sure you were safely returned to Pinehurst, so I'll tell him I wanted you to see your office one more time."

We enter the parking lot a few minutes later. My car is right where I left it, which probably was a mistake. We park in Grady's spot and get out. Grady takes my arm.

"Why is there nobody here?"

"We still shut down for two weeks at Christmas," Grady answers. "It's one of the few legacies that Trevor chose to maintain."

"At least it's something," I say.

Grady glances around the parking lot, then says, "There are no sound monitors in the old plant or out here, but there are cameras. Act like you're struggling to walk."

"After the evening I had, that won't be an act."

Grady puts his head down to hide his laugh from the cameras. I've already spotted three of them, two high up on light posts in the parking lot, the third mounted on the roof, focused on the front entrance. A few moments later, we're back in the old shop. Grady points to the far end of the shop, to a door that wasn't there when I worked here.

"That leads to the new addition. Trevor and his people have their offices in there."

"Show me."

Grady snorts. "My key doesn't work beyond here. It

hasn't since..." he pauses, thinks, then says, "four years ago. We'd already moved into the new addition." He uses his fingers to form air quotes. "The new world headquarters for Flanagan Furniture International. I had an office a few doors down from Trevor. Four years ago, they moved me back out here."

"Why?"

Grady winces. I see sadness in his eyes. "Neal, I don't know what you'll think of me after I tell you, but I sold my stake in the company to Trevor."

I can't believe what I'm hearing. I gifted Grady with fifteen percent of Flanagan Furniture on the day of his fifth anniversary with the company. It seemed an easy decision at the time, because without Grady we never would have become as successful as we were. I'd also gifted Trevor fifteen percent on his fifth anniversary. My financial and estate planner thought I was moving too fast, but I wanted Trevor to grow with the company just as I had Grady. It seemed ideal. My two top employees each owned fifteen percent of the company, Rosalie held a fifteen percent share, and I maintained fifty-five percent. The last thing I ever expected was for Grady to sell his stake.

When I don't respond immediately, Grady continues. "Violet's medical bills were unbelievable. She needed around the clock care. Hayley tried to help when she could, but the drive back and forth from Atlanta on her days off was wearing her out, and she'd only been married for a few months, so..." Grady pauses, takes a deep breath, and forges ahead. "Insurance only covered a few hours a week. I filed an appeal, but nothing happened. I tried working from home for a couple months, but quality suffered. I was at my wit's end when Trevor stepped in and offered to buy my fifteen percent. I knew how heartbroken you would be, but I was between a rock and a hard place."

"Did you consider taking an advance from the company, Grady? You were running things then, so it would have been easy enough."

"Rosalie made Trevor and me co-managers, on the same level. She was controlling your shares by then, and always knew how close you and I were."

What Grady doesn't say is that Rosie suspected that he'd known about Claire and me and turned a blind eye. He hadn't, not until I told him, but Rosie seemed intent on having someone to blame along with me. Grady was the most convenient target. I feel bad that his good name had been besmirched by my actions outside the company.

"Anyway," he continues, "Trevor and I sign the transfer agreement, then the next thing I knew, my ass was in purgatory." He motions with his chin toward our old offices. He pulled my access to everything except the old accounting system, which I still use to track the furniture repairs. These days I only see what Trevor wants me to see, and that ain't too damn much."

"Did Rosie know about that?"

Grady shakes his head. "She and Trevor grew close after you left. He made it a point to go by the house on a regular basis. He helped guide her through decisions she had to make regarding the company. She took her responsibilities as majority shareholder very seriously, and Trevor had her ear. That was when the company started changing direction. We began cutting back on how much furniture we made here in the plant. Trevor had already started cultivating connections in Southeast Asia, factory owners who could turn out cheap furniture fast, then slap the Flanagan name on it and sell it for huge profits. I pleaded with him to reconsider. The company had so much goodwill built up among customers. He showed me the sales projections under his reorganization. Profits were going to be astronomical, Neal."

"For the short term," I snap. I might've been away from the business world for a while, but my understanding of basic economics is still intact. If you build a following based on quality, then start making cheap products, there will be a period of time before your customers catch on. They'll continue to buy your product, assuming it's the same quality as before. When they realize you've substituted crap for quality they move on. Of course, by then, the company name is tarnished, sometimes to the point of no return.

"When Trevor refused to listen, I visited Rosalie. Trevor had shown her the same sales projections and she was excited. I tried to explain the long-term effects, but she told me I was from the old school. You and I both, Neal. She said we were from the old way of doing things. Trevor knew what was best, and she was going to listen to him."

"Rosie never understood business. She never wanted to."

"A few days later I got a call from Stephanie. She told me to butt out and not bother Rosalie anymore. She and Trevor would be advising her about decisions related to the company."

"Oh, great," I say. "That's a recipe for disaster."

There was a time when I'd hoped that Stephanie would assume leadership of Flanagan Furniture. She'd breezed through high school, majored in finance at the University of Miami, and even started her MBA at Florida State. She was smart and talented and headstrong as a mule. When she told me she wanted to try to make her own way in business, I supported her. She had some initial successes in real estate, made some money, lost some money, but overall was doing okay. Then she met Randy Mott. Randy Mott was the end of the Stephanie I'd always known. Randy was, according to Stephanie, a dreamer. I always found him to be more schemer than dreamer. First it was flipping houses. Stephanie was good at finding the properties, but when it came time to fix them up—Randy's responsibility—he proved inept at even the most menial tasks. They wound up hiring out all the work and killing their profit margin. Next was a retail store specializing in old-fashioned vinyl phonograph records. I read the newspapers. I knew vinyl was making a comeback. I also knew it was a few years from being profitable. When they brought it up over Thanksgiving dinner one year, I encouraged them to start small, maybe a rented storefront on a side street in Baltimore, where they'd settled to be near Randy's family. Instead, they signed a long-term lease agreement for space in a suburban shopping mall. Nine months later they declared bankruptcy for the first time. I paid thirty-one grand to dig them out. It put a dent in my retirement account, but that's what you do sometimes when you have kids.

"It sounds as if you were vocal with your concerns, Grady, and justifiably so. Did you ever worry that Trevor would fire you?"

"Nah," Grady shakes his head. "I was a black man in my fifties with a bad heart. I could sue his ass from three different directions, and he knew it, so we compromised."

"Compromised?"

Grady takes a few steps away, to shield his emotion from my view. "I agreed to stay on and oversee the shop, or what's left of it. Trevor agreed to fund my retirement. It was too late to start over by then, so I accepted the demotion."

Grady pauses to look across the mostly empty shop, then says, "I realize now how foolish I was."

I shuffle my feet as a few moments of silence pass between us. There's so much I want to know, like what Trevor is doing that has Grady so conflicted. Those questions can wait, though.

"Can I show you something?" he asks. We head back to his office where he pulls open a file drawer and gingerly extricates a handgun. Just the sight of it causes me to recoil. Grady sees my discomfort and sets it atop the file cabinet.

"You didn't know my old man was a cop, did you?" he asks.

"I don't think I even met your father."

"Back in the sixties he was Chief of Police in Claypool. It was a mostly-black community in the Panhandle." Grady uses his thumb to point over his shoulder at the gun. "That was his. As best I can figure it hasn't been fired since 1967. I don't even remember the make, but the guy at the gun shop knew all about it. He offered me seven-hundred-and-fifty dollars for it, but I turned him down."

"I'll give you a thousand just to toss it in the lagoon out back." My effort at levity goes unacknowledged, and I'm starting to get scared.

"Instead, I had him clean it up and make sure it still works," Grady continues. "Because on Christmas Day I plan to come up here, get it out of the drawer, take it out to the shop floor, and blow my brains out."

I feel my legs go weak. Grady Longacre has always been a rock of sensibility.

"Grady, I won't let you do that."

For some reason this makes him laugh. Laugh hard. So hard that tears come to his eyes.

"Neal, three days ago you didn't know who the hell you

were," he tries to continue, but the laughter is all-consuming. "And here you stand telling me that you're going to stop me from putting a bullet through my head. What are the odds, man?"

He has a point.

"For that matter," he says, still laughing. "How do we know that you'll even remember this by tonight?"

Another good point.

"If that's the case, then why don't you take me back to Pinehurst Pavilion? Maybe we can share a room. I'm sure they have a suicide watch."

My attempt at levity seems to have done the trick. The tense moment has passed, at least for now.

"Or you'll try to kick my ass again," Grady says in that singsong tone that reminds me of how he used to be.

"How about this, then," I offer. "Tell me everything that's happened, and we'll see if we can figure it out together."

Grady seems dubious of my offer, so I continue. "If I zone out again, you can kill yourself and I'll never be the wiser. But, if we can get to the bottom of what's rotten at Flanagan Furniture, then maybe we can find justice."

I can see that he wants a moment to consider my offer, so I venture back out to the shop, visualizing the men and machinery who used to fill this space. I wander to the far end where fractured and broken furniture awaits repair and rub each piece lovingly. God, we did good work in this place. Some of these pieces are over thirty years old, yet they're still beautiful. I think back to the days when we scrambled for every order, when the three guys working in the shop next to me would gather around our latest creations and admire them for a few moments before preparing them for shipment. Those were exciting times.

Behind me I hear a door open and close. I turn to see Grady enter the shop. He's holding something in his right hand, something small and dark. Damn, it's the gun. I raise my hand to beg him to set it aside, but before I say anything, I realize it's not the gun. I smile when I see that Grady is carrying something that used to be very near and dear to my heart.

"Where did you find that dinosaur?" I ask, pointing at the old-fashioned Rolodex.

"I pulled it from a dumpster not long after Trevor moved into your office?"

"Why?"

"You never know when contacts like these might come in handy," Grady says as he closes the remaining distance between us. He hands me the Rolodex. It's scarred and dented, but the lid opens easily, exposing yellowed cards full of names, addresses, and phone numbers. It's a who's-who, or perhaps a who-*was*-who of powerful and famous people who swore by our furniture. I'm sure a good percentage of them are retired or dead, but it doesn't matter. I flip through it anyway, recalling the names of men and women who called me their friend.

"You probably can't help me." Grady's words pull me from my reverie.

"Please, friend, just let me—"

He cuts me off with a swipe of his hand.

"Like I said, you can't help me. You're clear-minded today, sure, but who knows about tomorrow."

I nod. He's right.

"But since your brain is firing on all cylinders right now, would you consider making a call to someone who can help?"

He takes the Rolodex and flips it to the N's. He pulls one out and holds it up for me to see the name.

"Her?"

Grady nods.

"For..." I wave my arm in the direction of the shop floor. "For this?"

He nods again.

"Grady, I don't think you've thought this through. I mean, yeah, I could make the call, and I might even get through to talk to her."

"Then you should."

"But what you've described to me isn't the kind of thing that her people will involve themselves with."

"I realize that," Grady says. "But what if you can give her something that her people would jump all over?"

Grady has my complete attention. He motions for me to follow him.

"Are you up for a ride?"

I am.

"Then let's go. And bring that Rolodex card with you, because you're gonna need it."

ONCE WE'RE on our way, Grady pulls a manila folder from under his seat and hands it to me.

"This is just one piece of the puzzle," he says as he motions for me to open it. I do and find a death certificate from four months ago for a three-year-old with a name I can't pronounce. Before I ask any questions, I flip to the next page, a paid-in-full bill for services rendered by Hatcher Mortuary.

"This is so tragic," I say. "Friend of yours?"

"Trevor's housekeeper's son. He fell into Trevor's swimming pool and drowned."

"My god," I gasp. "That poor woman had to be devastated. Trevor, too, for that matter."

"The housekeeper is an illegal, and I'm talking in the traditional sense, like the many illegals who live and work here in Florida. She's from Cambodia. Are you starting to see a connection?"

I wasn't.

"Cambodia, Neal."

That's when it hit me.

"You said Trevor goes over there for work, right?"

Grady nods sagely but allows me time to draw my own conclusions.

"Are you thinking he's exploiting this woman somehow —no, Grady, I can't see it. The company is growing, Trevor is in a good position. Why would he risk it?"

Grady's gaze is on me, but he still isn't speaking, and I'm having a hard time putting this together. Trevor Stanley? The young man I hired wouldn't harm a fly. I'm starting to think that Grady has let his ill-feelings get in the way of good judgment. Maybe it's the reason he's been banished from the higher levels of the company. Perhaps before I do anything else, I need to talk to Trevor Stanley face to face, hear his version of things. Maybe Grady's suffering some lingering effects from Violet's passing. But wouldn't Claire have noticed? And if she had, wouldn't she have said something to me?

And why is Grady in possession of the death certificate for this poor woman's baby? Then, a really scary thought enters my mind: what if Grady was somehow responsible for the child's death? I put the brakes on this line of thought.

Grady is even less likely than Trevor to hurt another person. I decide to find out.

"Why do you have this?"

It's as if Grady was expecting this question. He answers straight away. "Trevor had me handle the arrangements. He made up this bullshit about being too close to the woman and her child, about how they'd lived with his family and how he and Vanessa were too broken up to—"

"Wait a minute, Grady. Do you think the child was Trevor's?"

"I asked her. The housekeeper's name is Sita. She said no, and the timing would agree. She was already pregnant when she arrived in America. She's learned enough English to be understood, but Trevor doesn't know that. She's been careful only to speak her native language in his presence. He doesn't think Sita can communicate everything that she's experienced, but trust me, Neal, she communicates just fine."

"What did she say?"

"That Trevor and Vanessa were forcing her to work for them. She was brought over to the U.S. with the promise of work and a better future but isn't getting any closer to living that dream. She was given a subsistence wage and a place for the boy and her to live, but little more. One Sunday a month off, no vacation, no healthcare. They don't hurt her physically, but she says she only wants to go back home, that as bad as things were for them in Cambodia, they're preferable to her life here."

I take another look at the death certificate. Questions bounce around my brain, but there are only two that need answers right now.

"Why would he entrust this responsibility to you, Grady?"

"Just to rub my nose in things, I guess. And to remind me that I'm nothing more than his boy these days."

The racial implication of Grady's comment isn't lost on me as I wait for him to continue.

"He pulled me in to tell me he wanted me to handle the funeral. It was the first time he'd spoken to me in weeks, and there's not been much said between us since. He has his circle of employees he confides in. A couple are college buddies. Two other guys are the size of football players. From what I can tell they're hired muscle. I never see them doing any real work. They were there when he called me in." Grady pauses, then as he continues, I see his eyes raging. "They stood behind him like in those gangster movies. The bastards were smirking at me. I started to tell Trevor to take care of his own mess, but he knows I'm desperate for my pension. I thought it was better to leave it that way."

This leads to my second question.

"As screwed up as this is, the only thing he's asked you to do is plan a funeral. What's this have to do with Flanagan Furniture?"

"Nothing really. The mess here is a whole other kettle of fish, but I thought it would be best if you saw firsthand the kind of snake Trevor has turned into. Hearing from Sita might be a good way."

There are other questions I want to ask, but Grady seems set on having me meet this lady, Sita, before he tells me anymore, so I oblige. He drives through Bradenton and across the Cortez Bridge to Anna Maria Island. Traffic is slow, as is always the case in December, and I take the opportunity to gaze at the Gulf of Mexico on our right side as we head south. Like most locals, Rosie and I never seemed to take advantage of our proximity to the beach, opting to swim in our backyard pool instead of fighting the hordes of tourists and day-trippers. I regret that decision now. Coquina Beach, on the island's south end, is tree-lined and reminiscent of a Florida of many years ago, despite the rows of SUVs that cram every nook and cranny of the dirt-paved parking lot. As we cross the drawbridge that allows boats to move from the Gulf to Sarasota Bay, I spot Beer Can Island and think of weekend boat adventures with friends. We enter Longboat Key, and the beach views give way to tall hedges and private drives designed to keep private beaches private, something that has always pissed me off. After a couple miles, Grady pulls onto one of those private drives and pushes the button on a callbox. The voice that responds is female, with an accent so thick that I'm not certain she even speaks English. Grady says his name and the gate opens.

The place – Trevor's place – is grand by beach standards. Probably four-thousand square feet, modern in style, and, though I cannot see beyond the front, I am pretty certain it backs up to the Gulf.

"How did you know she would let you in?" I ask Grady.

"I didn't, at least not for certain. I just assumed that with Trevor being gone, it was worth a try."

He's about to ring the bell when the large front door is opened by a slender, dark-haired woman who could be anywhere between thirty-five and fifty-five years old. Her tired eyes dance when she sees Grady, then go cold with fear when she spots me behind him.

"It's okay, Sita," Grady says softly. "This is Neal."

Sita's eyes dart from Grady to me, then back. She appears confused.

"Yes, it's Neal. The man I've told you about."

She gives me the once-over again before opening the

door wide enough to allow us entry. The floor tile in the entry shines brilliantly, undoubtedly the result of Sita's hard work. A Christmas tree, probably fifteen feet tall, dominates a front window. We pass quickly through a living room larger than my entire home and enter an airy kitchen. Sita points at the bar, indicating we should take a seat, then pulls open the door of an over-the-top Sub-Zero refrigerator and retrieves two bottles of water. Grady sees me giving the place the once-over.

"What are you looking at, Neal? Are you wondering why you never splurged for a place like this? It's obviously within reach for the head of Flanagan Furniture."

I shake my head in amazement. My highest annual salary was just north of one-fifty. I could've taken more, of course. The company was turning profits hand-over-fist, but I always figured that any money I left in the company coffers would be there later. I'd never considered that it would go toward buying a beach mini-mansion for Trevor Stanley.

Sita observes our discussion silently before speaking for the first time.

"Why you come, Mister?"

Her English is fractured almost beyond comprehension, but Grady is patient. "She understands the language much better than she speaks, but Trevor doesn't know that," he says to me. Then, to Sita, "I wanted Neal to hear your story. I've told him about Narith."

Sita's face dissolves into pain at what I assume is the name of her lost baby boy. She quickly turns and exits the kitchen.

"She'll be back," Grady says. He's right. She returns in a couple minutes with a small box. She lays it on the bar in front of her, opens it, and pulls out a photograph. When she holds it up for me, I see a young boy with many of Sita's same facial features. He is smiling, but it's the guarded smile of someone who is used to being afraid.

"He's beautiful," I say. She beams, nods her head, and begins speaking quickly, a stream of words that I think might be a pidgin of English and her native language, which Grady tells me is called Khmer.

"Tell Neal about your life here." Grady's tone is soft, but Sita still appears alarmed by the prospect.

"English... no good," she says haltingly.

"It's okay, Sita. You can trust Neal just like you trust me. And I know your English is much better than you're letting on. Remember our time together?"

Sita pours herself a glass of water and sits across from us at the bar. I notice that her hands are shaking but say nothing. When she speaks again, her English is more precise, less accented.

"He promise to let me go after funeral, but not happen." Sita tears up, but she doesn't bother to wipe them away. "I have sister used to live in Jacksonville, but don't know if she still there. I go to her or even back to my village. Anything better than this."

The despair of her words is real, in stark contrast to the artificial elegance of Trevor Stanley's home, and I start to feel something that goes beyond sympathy for the loss of her son. Emboldened by what she reads on my face, Sita continues.

"I have Narith out by swimming pool at night. I never leave him. He not allowed to go in water, but he like to be close. Mr. Stanley come and tell me to make drinks for guests. I start to bring Narith, but he say no, just me. I start to take Narith back to our room, but Mr. Stanley say, 'No.

Now!" real loud. I tell Narith to stay away from water and I be back soon, but he not do that."

The tears commence as poor Sita shares her heart-breaking story of loss. The death of little Narith was, it turns out, the sad culmination of several years of servitude at the hands of Trevor Stanley and his family.

"The men in my village give me to him," she says stoically. "There were others. They do it because he make his furniture where I come from."

I turn quickly toward Grady. He nods. "As we talked about before, Flanagan Furniture is now made in Cambodia. And Vietnam. And probably some other countries that I'm not aware of. It's made cheaply and sold at prices far beyond what it's worth."

"And profits are solid?"

Grady nods again. "Higher than ever, from what I can tell."

I'm starting to connect the dots. Trevor is taking advantage of the Flanagan name to market and sell cheap, foreign-made furniture on the American market.

"How long has this been going on?" I ask.

"It was gradual, but really ramped up after Rosalie passed."

Rosie would have controlled seventy percent of the company's decision-making, but she would never have green-lighted any changes that devalued the Flanagan name.

But after she died?

Our interest would've passed to Stephanie.

"Stephanie gave her voting interest to Trevor." I say aloud, getting a snort of derision from Grady.

"Stephanie *sold* her voting interest to Trevor," he answers. "As long as the checks keep coming, she's happy.

And trust me, Neal, given the profits the company has been clearing, I'm betting that Stephanie is very happy."

"While the Flanagan name comes to mean less and less."

Grady appears satisfied that I've unraveled the mystery.

But there's something else. Short-term profits are one thing, but the way Trevor has chosen to do business will eventually come back to haunt the company. It might take five or ten years, but eventually the Flanagan name will be synonymous with cheaply made imported furniture. I grab Grady's arm.

"Trevor is building up sales and profits so he can sell the company."

"You got it. I expect it to happen in the next ten to fifteen months."

Trevor really has become a snake.

But he had help. From my own flesh and blood.

"Grady," I say. "Why don't we take Sita to Jacksonville to find her sister?"

"I was thinking the same thing. We could leave right away and—"

"No!"

Sita grabs my arm just above the wrist. She's shaking again.

"Mr. Ballentine will find out and come get me! It will be even worse!"

I look to Grady to see if this makes any sense to him.

"Victor Ballentine?" he asks Sita. She nods but won't look at us.

"He comes by to check things for Mr. Stanley. When it's just me and him he—he hurts me..." she can't finish what she wants to say but pulls up the sleeve of her shirt. I see hand-shaped bruises on her bicep and feel the overwhelming desire to kick Mr. Ballentine's ass, whoever he is.

"Ballentine is one of Trevor's men." Grady says. "Director of Business Development. From what I can gather he makes frequent trips to Asia."

I've seen and heard enough. Sita isn't making this up, that much is obvious. Fear and intimidation have become as much a part of her daily existence as food and drink, and I want to remove her from the house even if she doesn't want to go.

"Sita," I say gently. "You can be safe. Just let us—"

There's a sound from the rear of the house. I hear it. Grady hears it. Sita does too, and fresh panic flashes across her face as she jumps up from her stool. It's the sound of a door being opened.

"Is anyone here?" Grady speaks quietly, but in the quietness of the house he sounds loud. Sita shakes her head.

"Grady," I whisper, moving close to his ear. "You didn't by chance bring your father's gun, did you?"

Grady didn't. I look around the kitchen, evaluating our options for defending ourselves. There's a butcher block holding a selection of knives, but it's across the room and whoever has entered the house is coming our way. We can hear his approaching footsteps. Yes, it's got to be a man, or a very large woman.

And then, the footsteps stop.

And he begins speaking.

"I'm inside."

Who is he speaking to?

"They're in the kitchen. What should I do?"

When there is no reply, I figure it out. He's speaking into a cellphone. He's not concerned that we hear him, either. Still seated, I reach out and pluck a wooden apple

from a bowl of wooden fruit in front of me on the bar. I'll
hurtle it with everything I have if necessary, which probably
won't be hard enough to propel it across the room. Years of
tossing lumber around the plant left me with a screwed-up
rotator cuff that doctors fixed the day after my fifty-first
birthday. They told me that I would regain full strength,
provided I did the rehab exercises they prescribed. I didn't.
By then, I wasn't throwing lumber around much anymore,
and the amount of paperwork I had at the factory kept me
away from the rehab center. The arm didn't hurt, but I
couldn't lob a lily across a ditch if my life depended on it.

I put the wooden apple back in the wooden fruit bowl.

"Okay, sir," we hear Ballentine say. "I'll take care of it."

The footsteps commence again, and I see that Sita has
retreated as far from us as she can get. She is terrified. I'm
starting to become alarmed myself.

But Grady has gotten to his feet and closed the distance
between us and the voice.

"Victor? Victor Ballentine? Is that you?"

A youngish man of perhaps thirty-five emerges through
the kitchen door. He would be considered handsome by
those women who like the upside-down triangle look of a
body builder who spends lots of gym time working on his
arms and chest, but none on his legs. He's wearing a navy
suit that fits snugly across the shoulders. His yellow tie is
loosened.

"Hey, Mr. Longacre." His voice is of a higher timbre than
I would have expected. Almost girlish, actually. Still, there's
no doubt that he could kick our collective asses to Key West
and back. He assesses each of us, his eyes resting a bit longer
on Sita than they should, making me reconsider grabbing the
wooden apple and letting it fly. The poor woman is terrified.

"We came by to see Trevor," Grady continues. He points to me and says, "This is Neal Flanagan, the company founder. He somehow got away from Pinehurst Pavilion, and I'm taking him back, but I thought that seeing Trevor might bring back some memories of—"

"Bullshit, Mr. Longacre."

Grady grows quiet.

"You talked to Mr. Stanley yesterday. You know he's out of the country."

I can see on Grady's face that he knows he's screwed up.

"I forgot... Victor. I've been so overwhelmed by the sudden appearance of my old boss that I... forgot."

Ballentine turns his apprising gaze upon me. A small smile plays across his face. "Good to meet you, Mr. Flanagan. Mr. Stanley speaks of you often."

The sudden courtesy catches me off-guard, and I'm about to express my appreciation when I have another thought.

"Who?"

"Mr. Stanley... Trevor Stanley. Surely you remember him, Mr. Flanagan?"

Now it's Ballentine who's off-guard. I decide to double down.

"Is he one of Stephanie's boyfriends? She's always bringing them by the house. I can't keep track of the names. Rosalie either, for that matter. We were just talking about that yesterday."

"No, sir, Trevor Stanley is... excuse me for a moment." Ballentine pulls his cellphone out of his jacket pocket and steps back through the door to the back of the house. We hear the back door open, and when it shuts again there is a collective sigh of relief. I rise from my seat for the first time, move to a window, and glance out.

"He's in the back yard," I tell the others.

"Quick thinking, Neal," Grady says as he produces a handkerchief and uses it to wipe perspiration from his forehead. I don't know what I was thinking by saying what I did about being here to see Trevor."

"Just stick by your story," I say quickly, keeping an eye out the window. "And Sita, don't you worry. We're going to get you away from here, safe and sound. If it doesn't happen today, it will soon."

Sita nods her understanding. When I see that Ballentine has left his spot out back, I scoot back to my seat at the bar.

"Mr. Stanley wants to talk to you." Ballentine says, extending the phone. I stare at it for a few moments, as if it might be a live grenade, then take it to my ear.

"Hello?"

"Neal?" I easily recognize Trevor's voice. It's a touch deeper, but still maintains that distinctive New England accent.

"This is Neal. Who's this?"

"It's Trevor, Neal. You remember."

"Sure!" I say happily. "How are you, Trevor?"

"Great! I can't believe we're talking. You've been... away so long, and now here you are. How did you manage to get away from Pinehurst?"

"Draymond decided to deliver the shipment to the Pentagon himself, so I went along. It's good to get out of the office sometimes, don't you think, Mitch?"

The line is quiet for a beat.

"Yeah... Neal, you're right about that. Are you enjoying your time with Grady?"

"I sure am. We're at a house right now, getting ready to leave a bid for some new kitchen and dining room furniture. I hate these small jobs, but the owner is some friend of Grady's, so I'll go along this time." I lower my voice for effect, then say, "The place is tacky, I'm telling you. The owner's personal tastes are shit, but we'll be able to make things look better. That's what we do, isn't it?"

Again, there is silence on the line. Across the room, I see Grady's eyebrows arch in surprise.

"Speaking of Grady, can I please talk to him, Neal?"

Wordlessly, I hand the phone to my friend.

"Hello, Trevor."

I can't hear what Trevor says, but Grady is playing up his own forgetfulness as they talk. The last thing he says before returning the phone to Ballentine is, "We were on our way there when I decided to bring him by here. I thought you would like to... yes, I completely forgot. That happens sometimes when I'm excited, and... no, he doesn't remember much of anything, just... okay, Trevor, I'm on my way."

Grady stabs at a couple buttons, then hands the phone back to Ballentine.

"Neal, it's time for us to get you back to Pinehurst," he says loudly, as if I can't hear well.

"Do we have time to meet Rosalie for a quick lunch?" I ask. Grady glances at Ballentine and shrugs. "His wife," he says quietly, as if I can't hear him. "She passed a couple years ago."

I think I see sympathy on Ballentine's face, but it disappears quickly. "I'll follow you back to make sure that you don't run into trouble," he says. "One of the maintenance guys at work is returning the old man's car to the garage at his house."

"That's fine," Grady answers. "Would you mind if I phone ahead so someone can come out and meet us. I get depressed going into the place."

"No reason why not," Ballentine says. "You know the number?"

"Yeah, they called me a couple weeks ago after Neal threatened to kick my ass. I saved it."

Grady scrolls through his cellphone before punching a button and waiting a moment until someone answers.

"Yes, is this the Manager's Office at Pinehurst Pavilion?" After a few beats, Grady says, "Then can you connect me with the Manager? This is Grady Longacre. One of your residents, Neal Flanagan, somehow got away and I'm bringing him back... yes, I'll wait..." Grady glances at Ballentine. "They're getting the manager."

"Hello... yes, Grady Longacre... he showed up two days ago... I know I should have called, but I assumed his daughter had checked him out and... yes, ma'am... yes, we'll be there in forty-five minutes. I was wondering if someone could meet us out front... yes, I've met her when I've visited him in the past. That'll be fine... okay, thank you."

After Grady puts away his phone, he glances at Ballentine before turning his gaze to me. "It's been fun having you around for a couple days, but it's time to go home."

I would've been more concerned had I not caught the sideways wink Grady gave me before turning back to Ballentine.

"I'm ready," I say. "It's meatloaf night, and Rosalie's meatloaf is as good as it gets."

THE SPEED LIMIT on Gulf Boulevard is thirty-five. Grady is going twenty-five.

"The Cortez Bridge opens for boats at forty-five after the hour," he says. "If I go slow enough, we'll have to wait. That'll buy us another ten minutes."

I nod, look over my left shoulder, and give a wave and bewildered look at the car behind us. Ballentine returns the wave.

"You are a genius, Grady Longacre," I say as I stare out the passenger-side window.

"If I were a genius, I would've had a better story for our appearance at Trevor's place. You're the one who saved our bacon back there, Neal. If Ballentine would have even suspected that you were in your right mind, I'm afraid to think of what might've happened."

"Will Sita be okay?"

"As okay as she can be for now," Grady says.

Sure enough, by the time we get to the Cortez Bridge, its center span is extended into the air to allow Sarasota Bay boat traffic to pass through. We idle and wait.

"That was Claire I was speaking to on the phone." Grady keeps his head down as he speaks, just in case Ballentine is able to read lips through a rearview mirror. "I'm hopeful she understands what is happening and can do something. If not, you might wind up back in your old bed at the nursing home. Either way, we'll figure something out."

"Call her back and make sure she understands."

"I'm afraid if I start making calls, Ballentine will want to know what's going on. Claire's a smart lady. Let's give her the chance to figure out a plan."

My stomach starts to ache as we get closer to Pinehurst. With so much going on – the changes at the plant,
Sita's situation – the last place I want to be is locked back
up. Grady makes a couple turns, and my home-away-
from-home appears on our left. The circle drive is short
and lined by palm trees, a fact I didn't notice as I made
my early morning escape. We pull up to a canopy that
leads to the main entrance. It's just before lunch, and
even with the windows up, I can detect the odor of insti-
tution food.

There is no sign of Claire.

"Grady?" I'm starting to get real nervous.

"If I make a run for it, Ballentine will be on us before
we get to Manatee Avenue," he says. "Let's pray that Claire
has figured something out."

As if on cue, the front doors slide open and a woman
appears. I strain to see if it's Claire. It's not.

She waves to us, then walks around the car to Grady's
side. She leans in closer as he lowers the window. Over my
shoulder I see that Ballentine has exited his car is coming
close to listen in.

"Mr. Longacre? I'm Sarah Rideout, the administrator.
Thank you so much for bringing Mr. Flanagan back. We've
been so worried about—"

Ms. Rideout pauses in midsentence when she sees or
feels Ballentine leaning in to listen. As she turns to face
him, she straightens to her full height, which brings her only
to his chest.

"Can I help you?"

Ballentine takes a step back before regaining his composure. "I'm with them."

"What's your relationship to the resident?"

"He's uh... he's my..."

"He's okay," Grady says. "He's a business associate of mine at Mr. Flanagan's former company."

Ms. Rideout still doesn't seem fully willing to accept Ballentine as part of the deal but relents after a few moments.

"Unfortunately, Mr. Longacre, the front entrance is closed at the moment. One of our residents is dealing with a terrible bout of diarrhea, and he made a mess just inside. It will take about twenty minutes to clean up. You can wait, or I can have one of our volunteers meet you at the side entrance and take Mr. Flanagan inside."

Grady glances at Ballentine. "I can wait if you want, Mr. Ballentine. There's no need for both of us to be stuck here."

"No chance," Ballentine answers quickly. "We'll take him to the side entrance."

"That'll be fine," Ms. Rideout says as she pulls a phone from her pocket and places a call.

"Joanne, would you please meet Mr. Longacre and his..." she takes another look at Ballentine, "...his work associate at the side door? They have Mr. Flanagan." She starts to disconnect, but reconsiders. "And, Joanne? Make sure that Mr. Flanagan is taken directly to his room and given the sedative we discussed."

Grady restarts the car and proceeds forward. I start to calculate the chances of making a clean break for it once we arrive at the side entrance. Sure, I can run, but I'm sixty-some years old. Ballentine is athletic, but musclebound. Probably slow for his age. I figure I can outrun him for twenty-five, maybe even fifty feet, but beyond that, no chance. "Grady," I say. "Is this the end of the line?"

"One way or another, I'll get you out of here. You've emboldened me by your presence, Neal. Two days ago, I was planning a scenario that had me sticking a pistol in my mouth and pulling the trigger. You've helped me move past that. Thank you."

"You're welcome, friend. I just hope I haven't punched my own ticket in the process. I don't know how long I can handle being back in there now that I'm clear-headed."

"Let me worry about that, but for now—"

I look at my friend to see why he stopped speaking. We've just turned the corner to the building's south side and he's staring gap-mouthed at the scene in front of us. Now I'm staring, too. Standing in front of us, decked out in pink slacks and a plain white blouse, sporting a tag with *VOLUNTEER* printed across it, and pushing a wheelchair, is Claire.

"Holy shit." Grady and I say at the same time. We pull to the curb. Grady shuts off the ignition as Claire pushes the wheelchair to my side of the car.

"Mr. Flanagan, if you ever run away like this again, our ladies' auxiliary will form our own search party. Do you know how *worried* we were?" Her accent is southern. Not Florida southern, more like Mississippi. Fake, but quite fetching, really. I've always been fascinated by women with southern accents.

The spell is momentarily broken as Ballentine approaches and opens my door.

"You must be the business associate," Claire says in her newly acquired singsong lilt. "I could use the help of a strong young man like you. Will you help me get Mr. Flanagan inside and undressed? He'll probably need the toilet, too."

It's a risky question that we all hope Ballentine answers to the negative.

"No way, lady. I don't touch naked guys unless they're me."

"Fair enough, then," she says, opening the car door. "In that case, Mr. Flanagan, let's get you back inside."

"Is Stephanie here?" I ask, continuing the ruse.

"Maybe so, Mr. Flanagan. If we can't find her, though, perhaps we might arrange for another surprise or two for you."

"I like surprises," I say enthusiastically as I get out of the car and take a seat in the wheelchair. As she bends down and adjusts the footrests, Claire winks and squeezes my thigh, and I feel myself blush.

"Unless you want to come in, I'll take him from here," she says to Grady and Ballentine.

"You can go in, Mr. Ballentine," Grady says quickly, pushing the envelope a bit further. "That place always stinks to high heaven at lunchtime. My stomach can't handle it until later in the day."

Ballentine, however, is already headed back to his car.

"I'm fine. Thanks, ma'am."

Ballentine starts his car and rolls a few feet ahead before stopping and looking at Grady who has also returned to his car. It's obvious that he won't leave until Grady does, so Grady complies, waving at Claire and me as he pulls from the curb. Satisfied, Ballentine follows. Claire and I wave farewell like a couple kids just dropped off at their college dorm for freshman year.

"See you around, asshole," I call out loud enough to make Claire giggle, but not loud enough for Ballentine to hear.

Then, they're gone. Claire bends over and plants a kiss on my cheek.

"Boy, am I glad to see you," I say.

"So, Ms. Rideout, the facility administrator, how did you get her to go along?"

Claire laughs merrily. Her dancing eyes make her look twenty years younger. "That was Genevieve Handley. She worked with me at the public library. Her husband's a resident at Pinehurst. I ran into her a few times when I came to visit you. After Stephanie got me barred, Genevieve would check on you and give me updates."

I'm touched by this gesture. And relieved that I'm seated in the passenger seat of Claire's high-mileage Chevy with Pinehurst Pavilion in the rearview mirror. As soon as Ballentine is out of sight, Claire wheeled me around the back of the building to where she stashed her car. We ditched the wheelchair and made our getaway.

"I have to admit," she says as we wait for a light to change, "it was kind of fun. Sort of like a TV detective show or something."

I take a few moments to tell her about Sita and the tragic death of her son. As I expect, Claire's ready to head straight out the Longboat Key and spirit Sita away to safety. Instead, we decide to wait until we hear from Grady, so we make our way back to Claire's place for sandwiches and romance. It's two-thirty, and we're under the covers, spent and satisfied, when her phone rings.

Grady.

"Ballentine followed me to the plant and stationed himself up the street for nearly an hour before heading off. That was too close, though."

Claire has the call on speaker phone so we can both speak.

"Let's go get Sita," Claire says firmly. "I don't want her

stuck there for a minute longer, especially with what that sleazeball Ballentine has been doing to her."

"I agree, but Ballentine or another of Trevor's cronies is likely to be watching for us," Grady replies. "We need to take our time."

"Fine, then," Claire says. "How about late tonight, maybe after midnight. We can be in and out of Trevor's place in ten minutes. Then we can..."

Claire's voice trails off as she realizes the problem with her plan.

Me.

"Don't leave me out," I say quickly. "I don't know how long I have before the fog returns, but I want to be a part of this."

"Unfortunately, that means that whatever we do has to happen in the light of day." The way Grady says this makes me think he's having second thoughts. He clears that issue up straight away.

"And if that's the way it has to be," he continues, "then that's the way it shall be. It's already mid-afternoon. Neal, while you're still alert, I'd like you to do something for me."

"Anything."

"Claire, fire up your laptop and have Neal take a look at the company website. After you've looked around a little, give me a call back."

I'm APPALLED by what I find.

The Flanagan website itself is beautiful, designed and maintained by someone who knows what they're doing. Granted, my knowledge of website development and the internet is ten years out of date, but I'm drawn to the ease with which I can navigate through the various options the website offers.

The first shock comes when I go to the tab titled *History of Our Firm*. It's not the oversized visage of *Trevor Stanley, President and CEO* that galls me, but the company background. I read it twice to make sure I didn't miss anything. I didn't.

Founder Neal Flanagan's focus on quality and craftsmanship has been expanded and improved upon by President and CEO Trevor Stanley. Under Mr. Stanley's leadership, the company has expanded many times over thanks to advancements in production techniques and value. What once was a small regional furniture manufacturer serving the needs of a few has evolved into a multinational company meeting the needs of many.

That bullshit is followed by more bullshit: glowing endorsements of Trevor's excellence from celebrities, business journals, and even a couple of athletes who Claire tells me are big stars these days.

"Notice what's missing?" I ask as I continue staring at the screen.

"What?"

"Endorsements from past customers. There's no one on this list who purchased our products during my years at the helm. No big hotel chains, no federal agencies." I click through to one of the product pages and understand why those endorsements are missing.

"Would you look at this stuff?" I'm speaking as much to myself as to Claire, but she leans in closer, pressing her front against my back and causing me for a moment to think of things besides furniture.

"The quality is about the same as they sell in the discount stores. Cheap particle board crap that you put together yourself." Things aren't much better on the page titled *Flanagan Signature Collection*, where I find the same crap with better-looking hardware. "At least this arrives fully assembled," I mutter as I close the laptop.

"Things change, Neal. Two office furniture stores here in Bradenton have closed in the past year. Maybe Trevor saw the handwriting on the wall."

I shake my head. "Our furniture was the best, and our customers knew it. They would never touch the stuff you find in those office warehouse stores. They wanted furniture that made a statement. Claire, back in 2004, twenty-seven senators were using our furniture in their Capitol Hill offices."

"Democrat or Republican?" she jokes.

"Both. And I can't begin to recall how many members of the House of Representatives were our customers. And to think that Trevor has kicked that segment of our clientele to the curb."

"Why would he do that? I don't know Trevor Stanley, but if you hired and trained him, he had to understand what the company stood for."

"Without seeing the books, it's hard to say, but based on what Grady told me, he's making this junk overseas. He probably has sliced the overhead to the bones and is focusing on short-term profits."

"Again, I don't understand why."

"To line his pockets. And to sell the company for a big profit. How computer savvy are you, Claire?"

"Not very."

"Me neither, at least not anymore, but I wish I could get a look at Trevor's compensation package."

"Can you Google it?"

"What?"

"Search for it on Google. They call that Googling it."

I reopen the laptop and begin searching, but fifteen minutes later, I'm still coming up empty.

"The company is privately held, so information like that doesn't have to be made public."

"But you're an owner, aren't you?"

"Technically, yes, but years ago I completed a power of attorney that assigned my decision-making responsibilities to Rosalie when I became incapacitated. I suppose, after Rosie passed, it was transferred to Stephanie."

"Maybe you should call her and—"

"That's the last thing I should do. She'll swoop in like a barn owl hunting a mouse. If the money's flowing like I suspect it is, she and Trevor are in a better place than they would ever be with me running the company."

"Then what should we do?"

Claire's question causes me to pause. There's so much happening, and while Flanagan Furniture and poor Sita are very important to me, nothing compares to the alone time I'm having with dear Claire. I set aside the laptop and take her hand.

"What I would really like to do is take you to the house and finish putting up the Christmas tree. Then we can eat leftover chicken, drink beer, and swim naked until I start to fade again."

Claire squeals with delight. "I haven't put up a tree in forever! Let's do it!"

IF CLAIRE FEELS the ghost of Rosalie Flanagan in the house, she doesn't say anything. We delight in hanging decades-old ornaments on the tree while we talk about Christmases past.

"Don't your kids visit for the holidays?" I ask.

She shakes her head wistfully. "I go there, usually. Last year I was at Amber's place in Houston. I'm supposed to spend this year with Keith and his family in New Jersey.

I am about to hang a yellow banana ornament that Rosie and I picked up in Maui back in ninety-four. I stop when I hear what Claire has just said.

"When are you leaving?"

She smiles and gives me a kiss on the cheek. "I called and cancelled yesterday. I want to be with you."

"Claire, honey, it's your family."

"They have their own lives. I'm just a fifth wheel." She glances around the living room, then locks eyes with me. "I'm right where I want to be, Neal Flanagan. Spending Christmas with the one person I always hoped I would be with."

We finish decorating the tree, then sit on the sofa and gaze at it. It's after six, and I suspect that my window of clarity will soon close, but I want to enjoy every second I have. Claire leans her head against my shoulder and takes my hand. We stay that way for a few minutes of silent bliss. I used to dream it could be this way. Claire and me. We wouldn't need anyone else. I shudder, and she squeezes my hand and asks if I'm cold. I'm not. What made me tremble was the realization that it really could've been like this. We both wanted it, but only one of us was willing to act on that want.

"I'm sorry I went back," I say.

Claire lifts her head and looks at me questioningly. Her pale blue eyes reflect the twinkling lights of the Christmas tree, the only illumination in the room.

"To Rosalie. I should've ended things when she found out. I should have ended things sooner than that. I wasn't happy, but I didn't want to..."

She smiles. It's a sad smile. "You had so much to lose."

"Not nearly as much as I lost by letting you go."

The quiet that surrounds us is equal parts sad and comforting. The sadness comes from what could've been, from the years we could've enjoyed each other just as we have for the past two days. The comfort comes from the realization that we have each other right now. It dawns on me how much right now means as you get older. As a younger man I was always looking ahead, counting down the days until the next big thing. Funny how the next big thing almost never seemed that big when it arrived. This, however, what is going on between Claire and me right now, it's the biggest and best thing. I don't want it to end.

"If it hadn't been for my kids, I don't know if I would've made it," Claire says quietly. Keith especially. He'd always caught the brunt of his father's temper. He suspected what Arch was putting me through. I spent time with Keith and Michelle up in New Jersey until I knew it was safe to come back."

"Why did you?" I ask.

"Come back?"

I nod.

She pauses for a few beats, then leans back against me and takes my hand in hers. "I came back hoping you might choose me."

Arch Tatum's vengeful response to our relationship comes flooding back. How he kicked Claire out of the house, going as far as throwing her clothes out onto the front lawn. He hired the highest-profile attorney in Tampa, then cut off Claire's access to their bank accounts before she was able to secure her own representation. He used his position as a community leader to poison Claire's name around town, to the point where no one would touch her with a ten-foot pole. Jobs that might've been within reach suddenly weren't. The few friends he'd allowed her to have disappeared. It had to be a hellish time.

And how did I respond to Claire's hardship?

The answer drives me to tears.

My weeping gives way to a headache.

And the headache to darkness.

I AWAKEN to a noise in the night. I sit up in bed. What bed? What sound?

"It's okay, sweetheart. It's me. I had to use the restroom."

Claire.

"Get back in bed," I say. "It's cold without you."

She giggles. It's a girlish sound that makes me wish I'd known her before.

Before she married Arch.

Before I married Rosalie.

"When does Arch get back from his trip?"

Claire's answer doesn't make any sense, really. Something about Arch not being around anymore.

"I wish," I say, and she giggles again as she crawls back under the covers. She snuggles in behind me the way we like best. Her hands are cold and send chills coursing through by body as she rubs them against my back.

"Sorry," she whispers. "I washed my hands. The water is slow to warm up."

"I'll warm your hands," I answer as I pull her arms around me. Claire sighs and burrows in deeper.

"Let's stay at one of the better hotels next time," I suggest.

"Neal, this isn't a hotel. It's..." Claire's voice trails off. Then after a moment she says, "You're right. A nicer hotel would be a good idea. Maybe one on the beach down at Anna Maria?"

"That would be too close to home. We would never get to leave the room."

Claire squeezes me from behind. "And what's wrong with that?"

I throw off the covers and start to get to my feet. "Oh, my gosh, I completely forgot."

I'm standing next to the bed. A clock on the bedside table that I've never seen before says it's three-forty-five in the morning. "We've got a shipment going out at five-thirty. Conference room furniture for the Treasury Department. I want to be there to make sure Draymond and the guys pack it right. Lloyd Bentsen has been a friend for a long time, and I want him to be happy."

"You don't need to leave this early, do you, Neal? Come back to bed for another half-hour."

I start to protest, but Rosie has a good point. I can get from our house to the factory in twenty minutes, so as long as I leave by five, I'll be fine. I crawl back into bed. Rosie snuggles up close behind me, which is strange because she always says she gets hot when we lie too close. Oh, well. It feels good so I stay where I am."

I AWAKEN AND KNOW EXACTLY WHERE I AM.

Claire is rubbing my shoulder. I roll over and see that she's fully dressed. There's a look on her face that I recognize as happiness muted by concern. I understand both.

"I'm back," I say, offering a smile. "I know who you are and where we are." I look around to confirm, then say, "When did we come back to your place?"

"It was about seven. You were complaining about a headache, but there was nothing in the medicine chest, so I brought you back here and put you to bed."

"That I don't remember, but everything before that... what a wonderful day. Thank you, Claire."

Claire appears happy. She leans closer and kisses my cheek. "I have two surprises for you."

"I can't wait." I pause, sniff the air, hoping to pick up the scent of bacon, but only detect Claire's sweet perfume. "Can I grab a banana or something quick to eat while you tell me? I'm starving."

"That's the first surprise. We're going out for breakfast."

"That's a grcat surprise. Where are we going?"

Claire runs her fingers through my hair. "Why don't you pick?"

I name three of my favorite breakfast places. Two don't exist anymore. The third has changed hands four times in the past decade. We laugh. Claire remarks that our situation is similar to that of a person who's been in jail for a long time and is finally returning home. We laugh some more, then I tell Claire to pick while I shower and get ready. She follows me into the bathroom chattering about other changes in Bradenton while I shave with the pink disposable razor she uses on her legs, then hop in the shower. By the time I'm out and dressed in one of my seersuckers, she's settled on a place called First Watch. "They're national, but based right here in South Florida," she says. That's good enough for me.

"What's the second surprise?"

"That one will have to wait. By the way, Grady is joining us."

"For the second surprise?"

"No," she laughs. "For breakfast. You and he have a lot to do today."

WE KEEP it light for the first few minutes, while we wait for our food. I'm munching happily on something the folks at First Watch call *Million Dollar Bacon*. It doesn't cost a million dollars, but I can almost understand why someone might be willing to pay that much; it's that delicious. Soon enough, though, the time comes to discuss the real reason for our morning get-together. I decide to get things rolling.

"What's on for today, Grady?"

"Do you still have the card I gave you yesterday?"

I pull the yellowed Rolodex card from my pocket and place it on the table.

"I believe that there's more than Sita," Grady says as I sip my coffee.

"At Trevor's house?"

Grady shakes his head. "It's just Sita there, but I believe that Trevor has been bringing others into the country under false pretenses, then placing them with his friends."

I nearly choke on my last bite of bacon. Has Trevor Stanley lost every shred of decency?

"Human trafficking," Claire asks. Her face has become as pale as I suspect mine is.

"I'm kept at arm's length, but I see things," Grady explains. "I believe that's one reason why Trevor had me arrange the funeral of Sita's son. By arranging the funeral, law enforcement might think I'm complicit in the overall scheme."

"Do you think he's aware that you might have information that could hurt his reputation?" I ask.

"He knows that I can figure things out."

"Like what?"

"Like four people on the manufacturing payroll that I've never laid eyes on."

"I thought you were cut off from seeing that stuff."

"I am, except for personnel involved with repair of the old stuff that comes in. The only people on our side of the place are Richie and me, but there have been a couple times when paychecks have been sent over for four people with names that sound like they're from a different part of the world. The first time I took them over to the tower to find out what was going on. Trevor happened to be in, and boy, did he ever blow up. Not at me, but payroll. He said they were prone to screw-ups and would be fired if they didn't figure things out. I took him at his word, but the same thing happened again four months later." Grady glances around the restaurant, then lowers his voice, and says, "I held the checks up to the light so I could see the addresses where the employees supposedly lived."

I can see he's very nervous about this discussion. "Would you prefer to continue this conversation in the car?"

Grady thinks that's a good idea, so we pay our bill. Claire says she should be heading back home. I very much want her to stay but realize that there could be a threat of danger, so I send her on her way. I get into Grady's car, and we pull away from the restaurant. He checks his rearview mirrors before saying, "The addresses on the paychecks are for a post office box in Palmetto."

Palmetto is a community just across the river from Bradenton.

"They all go to the same box?"

Grady says they do. "I went to the post office and made up a story about needing to see if one of our employees had picked up his mail. This was the day after the checks were mailed out. The postmaster didn't want to help me at first, but I was able to convince her that I was worried because the employee hadn't shown up for work. All she would give me was that the mail had been picked up, so the next month I took a sick day after checks went out. I hung out up the street from the post office and waited."

"Waited for what? You didn't know what these people looked like."

"True, but I had my suspicions. And, Neal, my suspicions were right. I wasn't there two hours before Victor Ballentine showed up."

"How do you know he was there for the checks?"

"Why else would he be in Palmetto? It's a nice place, but the post office?"

I see his point.

We pull into a McDonalds on Cortez Road. Grady takes a laptop from under the seat, opens it, and turns it on.

"Good WiFi here," he explains as he goes to the internet. I have no idea what he means by WiFi, so I watch silently as he types a few keystrokes, then a few more. He peruses what comes up, then turns it so I can see it. The language is foreign. The subject of the photograph is familiar.

Trevor Stanley.

"Watch this," Grady says as he opens a second screen and enters more keystrokes. The article that was in a foreign language is now in English. "The newspaper is in Cambodia. They did a big splashy story about how an American Industrialist," Grady uses air quotes to emphasize the last two words, "supports the Cambodian manufacturing industry and helps poor Cambodians find a fresh start in the United States."

I scan the article. Trevor is portrayed as a hero in Cambodia, providing work visas and new opportunities. It's the last two paragraphs that threaten to make me ill.

To those Cambodians who have escaped lives of hardship and poverty in the slums of Cambodia, Trevor Stanley is known as 'The Rescuer.'

"My family was gone, and I was expecting a child when I met Mr. Stanley," said one benefactor who asked that her name not be used. "I am now employed with Mr. Stanley's company in America. His family took me in and have made me part of their family. I couldn't be happier."

I turn away from the laptop and gaze out the window. There's no doubt who the anonymous Cambodian is supposed to be. And I know with all the certainty I can summon that Grady has figured out something that is appalling in its scope and intent.

Trevor Stanley is not the same young man I hired years before. That much is painfully clear. If everything Grady has learned turns out to be true, Trevor has evolved into a monster who is getting rich off my company and high off the praise of others who know not what he really is. I again produce the Rolodex card and ask for Grady's phone.

"It's time to make a call."

How HARD COULD it be to place a call to the Director of the FBI?

I'm discovering that it's pretty damn hard.

We head to my place for privacy. I begin by calling the 800-number Grady reads to me from the Rolodex card. A crisp male voice answers immediately.

"Director Newsome, please." I say.

"One moment."

I nod at Grady who is sitting across from me at the kitchen table. He's drinking my next-to-last beer. I'm having a sweet tea we picked up at Wawa. We wait a few seconds before another voice comes on the line. This one is female.

"Hello, Mr. Flanagan."

I smile and give Grady a thumbs up. "Director Newsome, thank you for taking my call. The reason I'm—"

"No, Mr. Flanagan, this is Christine Hockenberry in the Tampa field office. What can we do for you?"

I frown and give Grady a thumbs down. "I was hoping to speak to Director Newsome about a personal matter, Miss Hockenberry. Is there—"

"Agent."

"Excuse me?"

"It's Agent Hockenberry, Mr. Flanagan. I'm a field agent based here in Tampa."

"Sorry about that, Agent Hockenberry."

"Do you mind my asking what business you have with Director Newsome, sir?"

"Do you mind my asking how you knew it was me on the phone? Is my home phone bugged or something?"

"Caller ID, Mr. Flanagan. This is a landline that was established in your name in August of 1979."

"You didn't get all of that from Caller ID," I answer.

"We're the FBI, Mr. Flanagan. We know a lot."

"Do you know why I'm calling, then?"

Agent Hockenberry laughs. This surprises me. I figured FBI agents never laugh. They never laugh on TV. "I'm afraid you've got me there, sir. Why did you call?"

"To speak to Director Newsome."

"Ah, well that won't happen unless you tell me why you're calling, I'm afraid. That's the way we roll in the Bureau."

I'm starting to warm to Agent Hockenberry. She's got a little bit of attitude mixed in with her FBI demeanor. She's probably pretty good at what she does. I decide to trust her. I begin by telling her about my connection to Director Newsome.

"It started when we made a desk for her husband, Byron," I explain. "Do you know Byron?"

She doesn't, at least personally. I do, so I tell her about him. Rich kid, but not spoiled. As down to earth as anyone you'll ever meet, even though he deals in fine wines.

"He saw one of our desks in a friend's home, a man who happened to be a Wyoming senator. He ordered one just like it, except he wanted his initials carved into it rather than the senator's." I laugh at my little joke. Agent Hockenberry does too.

"Anyway," I continue, "one thing led to another, and we wound up building desks for most of the senior FBI offices."

"That's most impressive, Mr. Flanagan," Agent Hockenberry replies, and I feel she means it. "Are you calling to see if Director Newsome needs a new desk, because if you are, I can transfer you to our procurement division. They'll be able to—"

"Gosh, no," I say with a laugh. "Flanagan Furniture comes with a lifetime guarantee. She'll never need a new desk, unless she wants one of course."

I look across the table and see Grady shaking his head, reminding me that I'm wrong. "Oh, yes," I continue. "Flanagan furniture *used* to come with a lifetime guarantee. It seems that Trevor Stanley did away with that, along with a lot of other things."

"Is Mr. Stanley the purpose of your call?" the agent asks.

"Yes, ma'am, he is."

"How about this, Mr. Flanagan. Would you be able to come to our office here in Tampa tomorrow? Let's say, ten o'clock? It might be better to visit in person rather than over the phone."

"This line is bugged, isn't it?"

Again, Agent Hockenberry laughs. "Not that we're aware of, but I would still prefer to meet face to face. Are you agreeable?"

"Face to face?" I look across at Grady. He smiles and nods his head. "Yes, Agent, I believe I can do that. Give me the address and I'll see you tomorrow."

GRADY HAD BEEN GONE a half-hour when Claire returned to the house. She wanted to know everything, so I told her.

"Go with us to Tampa," I say as I pull her into a hug. I'm spending enough time away from you as it is."

"I was hoping you would ask," she replies as she pinches my cheek. "But aren't you forgetting something?"

"No, that doesn't happen until tonight," I kid, making light of my condition. "For now, my mind is completely present and focused on you."

She smiles, gives me a kiss on the lips, and says, "The second surprise?"

"Oh, yes!" I can hardly wait.

"I know you don't remember, but at one point in the middle of the night you mentioned that we needed to stay at a nice hotel."

I laugh, then remember that we were probably at Claire's place when I said it. "I'm sorry if you were insulted. I didn't mean—"

Claire shushes me. "Don't worry about it. You were remembering from before, back when we would meet at those cheap places on Tamiami Trail."

I grimace at the memory. "We did stay in some dives, didn't we?"

"It didn't matter. I was happy to be with you wherever and whenever."

"Even at the Bluegrass Siesta Motel?"

We giggle at the name of a long-gone roadside motel where we'd spent two or three afternoons, a place eventually dozed under to make room for a Cracker Barrel.

"Anyway, the second surprise of the day," Claire announces, "An evening at the Ritz-Carlton."

This does surprise me. "Holy cow, sweetheart, the Ritz? Really?"

Claire nods happily. "I had a little help pulling it off. Grady has friends there through work."

"I probably do, too. We did some lobby work for them over the years."

"The room is comped, courtesy of a man named Anthony Weedler."

"Amazing. Anthony was an assistant manager twenty years ago. So, he's still with them, huh?"

"He's the General Manager. Grady mentioned you were in town and looking for place for the night. Mr. Weedler insisted we stay there."

I guess Anthony doesn't remember the details about why I retired. That's fine. "What are we waiting for?" I ask

"It's not the Bluegrass Siesta, but I'm glad you approve. Let's get going."

I sigh with happiness as memories of our long-ago trysts come flooding back. Long lunch breaks that spilled over into the late afternoons. The lovemaking was sublime, for sure, but that's not the source of my remembrances. Claire Tatum, the timid homemaker from across the street, someone I'd considered little more than a shadow in the overwhelming presence of her successful husband, was, I learned during those meetings, very much her own woman. Arch's domineering might have muted her, but her spirit had not been snuffed out. Out of his shadow Claire was smart and funny and insightful. She told me of dreams she'd had as a girl, dreams that had been short-circuited when she married a man that she thought she knew but didn't. I'd done what I could, encouraging her to reach back and find those dreams, rekindle them, and allow them to again take flight. She'd laughed at first. After all, she was approaching her fiftieth birthday at the time. Later, though, at another cheap motel with another cheap motel name, she asked if I thought it was possible to go back, to reclaim those dreams. Of course, it's possible, I'd assured her.

And it would've been possible, had reality not gotten in the way.

DINNER IS SCRUMPTIOUS. The restaurant is new, but the location is one I know from before. It used to be a barbeque joint of some repute, but Claire tells me it recently morphed into the steak and seafood place it is today. She's wanted to try it for weeks but tells me she almost never goes out to places like this alone.

"Does that mean you sometimes go with other people?" I ask between bites of my Delmonico.

"Occasionally, but not nearly enough to get used to food this good," she replies. She has chosen Chateaubriand tips. "Isn't it heavenly?"

I sense that she is trying to steer the conversation away from my question about her dining partners, and that's fine. Claire is pretty and smart and has likely been the object of more than a few men's affections over the years. I hope she has had some nice experiences. She's earned them.

Her intuition is working overtime, as she picks up on where my mind has strayed. "I've dated a few men along the way," she offers. "They seem to fall into two categories."

"Rich and poor?"

She laughs. "That doesn't matter, really. I've lived without money for so long now that it doesn't mean anything. The two categories I run into are the hurters and the hurting."

"Wasn't that the name of a soap opera?"

"If not, it should've been. The hurters are men like Arch. They come across as suave and manly, but you quickly find that they're used to getting their way. Most have money, or at least want you to think they do. You're an hour into the first date, and they're already telling you how they'll protect you from whatever evil lurks around the next corner." Claire shakes her head. "I've learned to protect myself just fine, thank you. I say as much, but they're not programmed to hear that."

I'm not sure how to respond, so I take a sip of wine and wait for her to continue.

"The hurting, now they're even more dangerous. They unknowingly play into my maternal instincts. I want to save them from whatever hurt them."

"What is it that hurt them?"

"Divorces they didn't want, death of a spouse. Some have been downsized or outsourced from their jobs. I never realized how much men value their standing at work, Neal. I saw it in Arch, but I just assumed that was how he was. Why do you men put so much of your well-being on success at a job?"

I don't have an answer for her. It was important to me that Flanagan Furniture be successful. I'll also admit that I liked the personal attention it brought me. I was never one to namedrop, but there's a good feeling that goes along with being on a first-name basis with a senator or a bestselling author or screenwriter. I didn't start out in business with that in mind, nor did I shy away from it when it became a reality.

"The men who are hurting, they are so quick to latch on. They call and stop by unexpectedly. They're so in need of someone who is nice to them. It's just..." Claire pauses to gather her thoughts. "I'm not the same person I was before."

"You mean before you backed over my mailbox?"

We're laughing at that memory when the waiter comes by to refill our wine glasses and leave dessert menus.

"You unlocked something in me, Neal. Before you I would never have been able to stand up to everything that Arch put me through."

"I wish I had chosen to be there with you."

Claire waves off my sentiment. "I was a big girl. Even if I had known going in how everything would turn out, I would've continued to see you."

"Still, going back to Rosie was... it hurt so much."

"What hurt, Neal?"

"Being where I was and knowing what could've been, if..."

"If what?"

"If I had been a stronger man."

She reaches across and takes my hand. She kisses it gently and pulls it to her cheek. "You're here now."

"Tell me about your road? What have the years been like?"

"Are you kidding?" She says as she flags down our waiter. "That's a heavy topic that we'll save for another day. I'm ready for dessert and a night with the man of my dreams."

"I just don't know how you can say that," I protest. "The man of your dreams left you high and dry. He watched as your husband kicked you out and made sure everyone knew what we'd done."

"You did what you thought was right at the time. I never faulted you, Neal, and do you know what else?"

I don't.

"I never stopped loving you."

I'm AWAKENED from my dozy state by a knocking sound. When I open my eyes Claire is beside me, head propped up by her left hand, looking down in the dim luminescence.

"Is someone knocking on the door?"

She giggles and points to the wall above the headboard. "The folks next door are celebrating like we were earlier."

"We didn't make that much noise."

"Don't sell yourself short, Mister," she says as she strokes my hair. She leans closer and kisses my forehead. Her touch, her kiss, her closeness seem amplified somehow. I suspect it's the wine.

"It's eleven thirty," she whispers.

"Really?"

"Really."

That means I haven't faded away like every other night. The realization makes me laugh aloud.

"Maybe I'm kicking this Alzheimer's thing after all."

Rather than answer, Claire kisses my forehead again. Then my nose. Then my lips. I kiss her back.

I AWAKEN AND KNOW EXACTLY WHERE I AM.

The Ritz Carlton.

I hear Claire moving around in the bathroom. Getting ready for our big day in Tampa, undoubtedly. I stretch, roll over onto my belly, and glance at the clock.

Eleven-fifteen.

Eleven-fifteen?

I scramble from the bed just as the bathroom door opens. It's not Claire.

It's Grady. There's a worried look on his face that dissolves somewhat when he sees me standing in front of him.

Then I remember I'm naked. I grab the bed sheet and attempt to pull it from the bed. It snags and I go scrambling to the floor. I'm okay, but this is embarrassing as hell. Behind me I hear Grady begin to laugh. He goes back into the bathroom and returns with a Ritz Carlton bathrobe that I gratefully accept.

"It's eleven-thirty," I say as I tie the robe.

Grady nods. "We missed our meeting."

"Why didn't you wake me up? And where's Claire?"

"Claire ran back to your house to get some of your things. She's also picking up something to eat. We woke you up, Neal, but you weren't... you."

I sense what Grady is alluding to and wonder if it had anything to do with my extended lucidity the night before. Or the wine. We certainly drank a lot of wine. Then, I realize that none of that matters. Grady was depending on me to save Sita. And maybe save Flanagan Furniture.

"I'm sorry, Grady."

"You shouldn't be sorry," he shrugs. "Now get yourself ready to go. Check-out time is noon."

"I'll call the FBI and see if we can get a later appointment."

"We already did. Claire and I both tried. No one is taking our calls."

Lunch is subdued. We eat sub sandwiches and chips in a Bradenton park while we plan how to proceed. I feel terrible about oversleeping. The others do their best to console me, but I can see they're saddened by the change of events.

"We can still save Sita," I offer.

"Not during daylight hours," Grady says. "Trevor's guys are probably keeping a close eye on things. I went to the office this morning after we were unable to wake you up. Victor Ballentine came over to my office twice. I've never seen him in that area of the building before."

"What did he want?"

"Nothing really. Innocuous questions about security and that kind of stuff. He very pointedly asked if I'd been to see you anymore. Then he said he was thinking about going by the nursing home himself, just to check on you."

My stomach lurches at the possibility.

"I don't think he will. I suspect that Trevor told him to keep his thumb on me. He said something about going out to check Trevor's house, making sure no one else broke in."

"Broke in?"

"That's what he said. I got the message. Stay away."

I glance at Claire. She's been listening but not saying much. "What do you think?"

"You're my main concern, Neal. I think we pushed you too hard last night. I should've insisted that we cut back on the wine and turn in earlier."

"It was one of the best nights of my life," I answer.

"I'm just happy it wasn't the last night of your life," she says. "I was so scared this morning. When I was able to wake you up for a few moments you were not aware of who I was or where you were. I waited a half-hour, but things weren't any better."

Grady wads up the wrapper of his sub and gets to his feet. "I need to get back to the house, just in case Ballentine is checking up on me." He looks at me, smiles warmly, and says, "I love you Neal Flanagan. Your return has been just the medicine I needed, and I'll be forever grateful. Even if we can't get this mess with Sita straightened out, I know I'm going to be all right."

I'm touched and encouraged by my friend's words. I thank him and am standing to see him off when I spot three people coming toward us from the park entrance.

Victor Ballentine I immediately recognize. There's a

look of satisfaction on his face. He's smiling, and I know why. He has just captured his prey.

The man flanking him on his left, I don't recognize. He's wearing a nice suit and has the seasoned tan of a person who probably enjoys Caribbean vacations and frequent rounds of golf.

And on Ballentine's right, Trevor Stanley. He appears perturbed, as if the family dog just crapped in the middle of his dinner party.

Their backs are to the three, so Claire and Grady are unaware of their approach.

"Things are about to become difficult," I say softly as I begin walking toward our visitors. When I'm within arm's length I extend my hand.

"Trevor, it's great to see you!"

My forthrightness has caught Trevor off guard. He awkwardly shakes my hand. "Neal, I thought you were back at Pinehurst Pavilion."

He obviously knows better or he wouldn't be in a public park at lunchtime. How much he knows is still up in the air.

"I just got back from Washington, Trevor. I told you I was going." I become stern as I say, "Haven't we talked about you making more of these trips? I was just telling Grady the other day that I'm starting to grow tired of long flights."

Trevor blinks several times and I'm starting to think I've snowed him. His gaze shifts from me to Grady, then to Claire, and finally back to me.

"Bullshit."

"Trevor, you know better than to talk to me that way."

He flashes an ugly grin. "You think you've pulled the wool over on us, Neal, but I know better."

"You're embarrassing yourself, Trevor. In front of these

gentlemen." I offer my hand to the suntanned one. "Neal Flanagan, and you are?" He looks to Trevor briefly, then back at me. He doesn't speak. I shrug and turn to Ballentine.

"I'm Neal Flanagan. Are you Trevor's father?"

In lieu of a response Ballentine shoves me to the ground. The grass is thick and soft, the Saint Augustine variety that's so common in Florida, so I'm not injured. What I am is aware. Aware that the gig is up. Something's about to happen, and it's about to happen to me.

I'm still on the ground when Trevor says, "I don't know how or why, but you seem to have returned to your senses, Neal."

There's no need to say anything in response, so I don't. Claire, on the other hand, has plenty to say. She rushes over to help me up, swearing and cussing a blue streak at all three of them.

"You're the lady from the nursing home," Ballentine says, ignoring her verbal onslaught. He turns to Trevor and says, "She met us at the car with a wheelchair."

I'm standing now. I brush off my suit and straighten my jacket. Grady comes and stands next to me. Claire takes my other side and grabs my hand.

"This is Dr. Patterson," Trevor says casually, as if we're discussing the weather. "He runs a long-term care facility in St. Petersburg. You're going there to be evaluated, Neal."

"The hell he is," Claire snaps. She holds my hand tighter.

Trevor continues. "And Grady, you're fired. You've been a thorn in the side of this company for too long. It's a sorry way to show your appreciation to me for keeping you around after you became useless to the company."

I glance to my left and am surprised to see Grady grinning like a maniac. Then, his hand goes to the pocket of his windbreaker and I know why. He pulls out his father's gun and is raising it when Ballentine lunges at him. Grady is smart and nimble enough to sidestep the attack, but Ballentine still is able to spin him around with just enough force to throw Grady off balance. Five seconds later Grady is on the ground, and Ballentine has the gun tucked away in the waist of his pants. That's when I know things have gone far enough.

"Do what you have to do, Trevor. Just leave Grady and Claire alone."

FROM THE FRONT passenger seat Dr. Patterson tries to engage me in conversation on the drive to St. Pete. He brings up the weather, the upcoming holidays, and even Buccaneers football. I say nothing. Ballentine is driving and doesn't speak much either. Trevor didn't make the trip.

It's evident that my silent treatment is irksome to the good doctor.

"You'll be evaluated and placed appropriately," he snaps. "Cooperate if you want or be an obstinate ass. It's up to you."

The results will probably be the same, I think but don't say. Patterson opens his briefcase and holds up some official-looking documents. "You're fortunate that Mr. Stanley and your daughter are such close friends."

I work to keep a straight face. Of course, they're friends. Trevor needs Stephanie's share of the company. Stephanie and Randy love the steady income Trevor provides.

"She signed off on your transfer to my facility. It's a lot more secure than that warehouse they had you in before."

It's time to speak. "Who is the big ugly guy driving? Is he a chauffeur? Are we headed to the airport?"

I can see Ballentine's hands clench on the steering wheel. He catches me looking at him in the rearview mirror. His eyes are dark and foreboding, not a person I would want to meet in an alley at midnight. He won't say anything, though. The floor is Patterson's, and he's intent on bragging about his success.

"My credentials are impeccable, Mr. Flanagan. My practice flourishes, and I've built up quite the reputation for my work with uncommon patients like yourself."

I'm wondering what he means by 'uncommon patients.' Perhaps people who emerge from dementia? Or is he referring to old men who suddenly reappear and start causing trouble? I would love to ask, but instead say, "Are you a chiropractor? My back has been killing me. I keep telling Betsy to find me a new desk chair, but she never seems to get around to it."

"We see patients who emerge from Alzheimer's for short periods. Not many, but there are a few." Patterson turns in his seat and looks back at me. "I suspect that your emergence is for a longer time. Lucky you. You're fortunate to get one more chance to experience life. It's just too bad that you had to screw it up."

I don't reply. I close my eyes, instead, and relax my head against the seat. Most people would get the hint that I'm not talking. Patterson is oblivious.

"You probably regress in the evenings. We call that sundowning, Mr. Flanagan. Or late-day confusion. It's more apparent in early-stage patients. How far do you regress?"

"Can we stop for a minute? I need to make a phone call?"

"No time for that now, sorry. When we get to my facility, would you be amenable to me conducting a few tests? It might be helpful to the field."

"What kind of tests? I'm scheduled to renew my driver's license in February. Can you give that?" I allow my voice to grow angry. "And you never told me who the asshole is who's driving the car. I don't like his looks."

Ballentine is getting edgy. His mouth is twisting and turning, and his eyes have become slits. I'm ready to take another run at him when I remember that he has Grady's gun tucked into his waistband. He probably won't shoot me, but it pays to be smart. Patterson continues to act as if he doesn't hear my responses. He's still back on the question of running tests on me.

"No problem, Mr. Flanagan. I'm sure we can get your daughter's approval for a full battery of cognitive tests."

The car grows silent as we cross the Skyway Bridge into St. Petersburg. Fifteen minutes later we pull up to a plain-Jane block and glass two-story building a few blocks from Tropicana Field. The sign out front identifies it as the Patterson Long-Term Care and Rehabilitation Center.

"If you're so renowned why is your building so shitty looking?" I ask.

"This is just the annex, Mr. Flanagan. Our main facility is on Fifth Avenue near the waterfront. You'll never see it, though."

We pull into a reserved parking space and I'm escorted inside. As we're buzzed through two thick doors, I'm reminded of the police dramas I used to enjoy. This place isn't a rehabilitation center. It's a prison. Just inside the second door we're joined by two orderlies, a male and female. They nod an unsmiling greeting at Patterson.

"Put him in two-oh-eight," the doctor says before

turning away. "You'll see me soon, Mr. Flanagan." He and Ballentine head for the exit. I'm escorted to an elevator. The orderlies flank me as we ride up. The male is scrawny and disinterested, but I suspect that he must be competent, or Patterson wouldn't have left me in his care. The woman scares me. She appears to be in her early forties with short arms and a butch haircut. I'm pretty sure she could kick my ass, so I don't try anything.

On the second floor they take me to a room that is much like the one I left behind at Pinehurst Pavilion. A bed, a closet, a bathroom. No television. No chairs for visitors.

"Get out of that faggy suit and put this on," the scrawny orderly commands as he shoves a hospital gown in my face. "Everything off. Socks, underwear, everything."

They stand by while I comply. I consider making a comment about the way they watch my every move, even while naked, but don't. There's a clock on the wall: five-fifty in the afternoon. My clear period will likely be coming to an end soon.

"Get in bed and wait," Stocky says. "We'll be back with your supper in thirty minutes."

"And don't try any shit, because we'll be watching," Scrawny warns as he points at a camera on the wall near the ceiling.

And then they're gone. They've left the door open, so I don't close it. Instead I go to the window. It's one of those double windows that slide sideways that you see in hospitals and other institutions. I shove it to the left, but it doesn't move. I shove harder and feel it give just a little. Then I grab it with everything I have, and it opens about a foot. I look out and down. The ground is about twenty feet below me.

But there's a fire escape.

I squeeze myself through the tightness of the open window, step onto the fire escape, and feel the wind blowing up my hospital gown. It's dusky, but not completely dark. If someone happened to be walking by, they would see my backside and most everything else on full display. I step gingerly across the fire escape and onto the ladder. Then I'm on the ground. The grass is dewy and muddy from rain, and I have no shoes. I'm not sure where I am, so I start walking. The area is gritty, not a place I would consider walking through after dark, but what choice do I have? Several people pass me, but don't acknowledge my peculiar appearance. That says as much about the area as anything. After twenty minutes of walking I come to an underpass. There are shopping carts and baby strollers overflowing with all matter of stuff. Beyond them, further under the road, I see movement. People. Undoubtedly homeless. I hear snickering and a couple threats tossed out of the darkness. I'm probably about to get my ass kicked, but what the hell.

"Anybody got a cellphone I can use to make one call?"

Several more insults come my way. Then a woman steps out into the gloaming. She might be fifty or she might be thirty.

"You got any money?"

I nearly laugh.

"They took my clothes. And my money," I add, hopeful of pity.

I get pity. The woman holds out her phone. I take it, then remember that I don't know Claire's phone number. Grady's either.

The only number I do know is my old home number.

I dial it.

And Claire answers.

"Come get me. I'm at..." I pause and look at the lady

who loaned me the phone. She tells me where we are, and I tell Claire.

"I might not be... you know... when you get here. I'm already starting to feel different."

"We'll find you, darling. Just stay where you are."

So, I do.

CHAPTER TEN
THURSDAY, DECEMBER 17

I awaken and know exactly where I am.

Damn.

Damn, damn, damn.

I'm not at my house.

I'm not at Claire's place.

I'm not at Grady's place or the Ritz Carlton.

I'm in the room I escaped from yesterday. I'm in the bed, restrained by straps across my legs and torso. My mind is sharp, at least up until the point when I called Claire from the underpass. Beyond that, my memories are bits and pieces.

Did Claire come to get me? I don't remember seeing her.

I do remember punching the stocky orderly, though. That happened outside, in the darkness, on a street someplace. I remember seeing her hit the ground hard. My memory from there grows dim. There was a van, blue I think, with a name on the side. I was placed in the back, in a cage of sorts. Someone pushed me into a shower at some point.

That's it.

Damn.

Bright sunshine streams in through the window I was able to open last night. There's a bar and padlock on it now. As I consider my situation, an orderly comes in with a breakfast plate. She's not one of the ones from yesterday. She has kind eyes.

"Let me up."

"You know I can't do that, Mr. Flanagan." Her voice has a southern lilt, Tennessee or Arkansas probably. Definitely not deep south.

"I need to use the restroom."

"Go ahead. You're wearing a diaper."

I squiggle my backside around on the narrow bed and confirm what she's just told me. Yep, a diaper.

"Would you like some oatmeal? I've got eggs and toast, too."

The last thing I want is to take their food, but I'm hungry as all get out. The sub sandwich at lunch yesterday was the last thing I remember eating. The orderly raises the bed so I'm sitting up, then pulls up a chair and spoons out some oatmeal. I accept. She smiles. I'm tempted to ask what happened last night, but the camera on the wall catches my attention. Even if she's Mother Theresa, this girl isn't going to jeopardize her job by saying something that will probably be overheard by a higher-up. I remain quiet. She continues to feed me until I've eaten everything. She offers me water to wash it down, then packs up the tray and heads for the door.

"You have guests coming by in a few minutes," she calls back.

I don't reply, but my hopes are high. Did Grady figure a way to get in to see me? Claire? Maybe the FBI found out what happened and are on their way to get me out. I decide to say little until I know who's coming through the door. The time ticks away slowly. Seven-thirty becomes eight. Eight becomes nine. My bladder is screaming, but the last thing I'm going to do is soil myself. Then, at nine-twenty, the door opens with a flourish. It's that quack Dr. Patterson.

"Right through here, folks."

He's followed by my daughter, Stephanie and her useless husband, Randy.

And my grandson, Michael.

My heart leaps when I see how big he's gotten. He's not a boy anymore. Michael Mott is a man. I want to acknowledge how happy I am to see him, but hold back. I probably couldn't have resisted had he been alone. Seeing Stephanie, though, gives me pause. There's a look in her eyes that could scare lesser men. Stephanie Flanagan Mott is not happy to be at the Patterson Long-Term Care and Rehabilitation Center. And Randy? Who cares?

Dr. Patterson is all rainbows and smiles as he approaches my bed.

"Good morning, Mr. Flanagan!"

"Good morning, Draymond."

Patterson appears confused.

"Draymond used to work for him," Stephanie says. Then, coming closer, she says, "Hi, Dad, how are you?"

"I seem to be stuck here, Betsy. Can you help me?"

Stephanie's eyes grow cold.

"Who's Betsy?" Randy asks.

"She was his bitch of a secretary," Stephanie says indignantly. "She was old and ugly, and I can't believe he thinks I'm her."

"As I mentioned on the phone, Mrs. Mott, your father

has been having periods of lucidity. There's a very good likelihood that he's faking his condition as we speak."

Stephanie reaches over and takes my hand in hers. I'm strapped in, so she can't move it far. Strangely, I feel nothing when she makes this gesture. Her hand is cold and impersonal, just like her demeanor after Rosie told her about me and Claire.

"Dad, do you know why you're here?"

I take a furtive look around the room but say nothing. I lay my head back, fart loudly, and close my eyes.

"He's not having a good morning," Patterson says. "As I was telling you on our way in, he's deemed a flight risk after what happened last night."

Randy laughs. It's a dry, ugly sound, devoid of humor. "This place must be a real shitbox if an old man like him can just walk out."

I can see that Patterson has taken this personally. His eyes flare, but he's looking at me so the others can't see it. "Quite the contrary, Mr. Mott. Your father-in-law pried open a secure window and escaped down a fire escape. It's the first time we've had someone leave the annex unaccompanied since we opened, and you can be assured it won't happen again."

Randy shakes his head as if he doesn't believe the doctor, then pulls out his cellphone and gives it his full attention. Michael, standing behind his parents, is taking everything in, but not saying anything. Patterson eventually leaves us to go wherever unscrupulous physicians who are on the take go. Now it's just me and my only remaining family.

Yippee.

There are no chairs, so they are forced to stand around me and gaze down. I feel like I'm in a coffin at my own funeral. Stephanie is on one side, Michael on the other. Randy continues to fiddle with his phone.

"You've had quite a week, haven't you, Dad?"

I open my eyes and look at Stephanie. The years haven't been kind to her. She's got more wrinkles in her forties than her mother did in her fifties. Her hair is cut short, too short to retain any vestige of femininity. When you toss in all that and her rail-thin frame, she almost looks like some street corner junkie, if there still is such a thing. That saddens me, but the show must go on.

"It's been a busy week for sure, Betsy. Did you get the sales reports for July done? I need them for my meeting with Trevor and Grady at noon."

"I'm not Betsy, Dad. It's me. Stephanie."

I nod but don't reply. Randy speaks from behind her. "How long do we have to stay?"

"Dammit, Randy, I told you we would catch the six o'clock Delta flight back to BWI. I need to know how Dad is doing, though, so if you don't mind."

Randy doesn't seem to mind. As long as he has his cell-phone he seems as content as a pig in slop. Come to think of it, pigs are an apt description of Randy Mott, provided the pigs aren't offended by the comparison.

"Did you see how grown up Michael is, Dad?"

I turn to look at my handsome grandson and am struck by his eyes. They're so kind, so gentle. I decide to throw caution to the wind.

"Hi, Michael, how's the job search?"

He seems surprised that I remember. Stephanie snaps to attention, and even Randy looks up.

"Nothing yet, Grandpa. I have an interview on January third with an internet marketing firm, though."

"You know a lot about the internet, do you?"

He smiles. "Maybe too much. I love doing troubleshooting and cyber security. You probably don't know much about that.

I shake my head and feign weariness. "Not really. What I really wish is that you would come work with me at the factory. Lean in and let me tell you something."

Michael puts his ear a few inches from mine, but I make sure that my voice is loud enough for the others to hear. "It was always my hope that your mother would take over the company. She could've done a great job at it, but she married your father. He doesn't work very hard, does he, Michael? Your father, I mean?"

Michael turns red. He looks up at Randy who is giving me the evil eye. "The old son of a bitch never appreciated me."

"The company is in a good place now, Dad," Stephanie says, ignoring my dig at her husband. "Trevor has done a magnificent job."

We endure one another's company for forty-five minutes. Michael tells me about some of his college classes. I play the part of a man in the throes of middle level dementia. I alternate my performance from somewhat lucid to dozing indifference. I can tell that Stephanie is growing weary of the visit, and just a few minutes before eleven, she says, "I'm going to go find a bathroom, then we can leave. Maybe Delta has an earlier flight to BWI."

"I'll check," Randy says with more enthusiasm than he's shown all morning. He begins pushing buttons on his phone while Stephanie steps out. After a few moments he mumbles something about having to call the airline. He places his call and begins gabbing loudly with a ticket agent. It's just me and Michael.

"Sorry you're not doing well, Grandpa," he says. "I miss the fun we had when I was little."

We're having a moment. It might be the last we ever have, unless I do something.

But what?

While Randy continues to ramble on to the Delta agent, I allow saliva to drip from my mouth onto my chin. Michael, being the kind of young man I always knew he would become, grabs a tissue and moves in close to clean me up.

"Stay," I whisper.

Michael's eyes open wide. I'm afraid I've spooked him. He glances at his father then at the hallway door, then leans closer and continues wiping my chin.

"I need you. People are in trouble."

Will Michael take my words seriously, or will he consider them the renderings of misfiring synapses? I want to say more, but Stephanie returns.

"Did you find an earlier flight?" she asks Randy. He holds up a finger, finishes what he was saying to the Delta rep, then puts the phone away. They have three seats on the one-twenty. If we hustle, we can just make it."

Stephanie looks from Randy to me, then back to Randy. "Let's go."

Stephanie leans close as if she's going to kiss me, then reconsiders. "Bye, Dad," she says quietly. "Sorry things turned out like this. Maybe it's payback for how bad you hurt Mom."

Randy overhears what she says and flips me the bird. Michael kisses my forehead. "Bye, Grandpa."

My heart sinks. He didn't believe me. They're gathering their coats when Michael suddenly says, "Mom, can I stay for a couple days? It's been a lousy couple weeks with finals and job hunting. I would love to hang out at Grandpa's place and spend some time at the beach."

I'm all ears for Stephanie's response.

"When do we have guests at the old house again, Randy?"

"Not until after Christmas."

Stephanie eyes Michael. "No parties?"

Michael crosses his heart. "Promise."

"And you have to clean up," Randy interjects. "Neal was at the house for a few days. It's hard to say what kind of mess he left behind. If you're going to be there, I'll tell the maid service that we'll make sure the place is ready."

"Deal," Michael says happily. "Thanks."

Stephanie opens her purse and holds out some bills. "Here's some money for an Uber. We don't have time to take you down to Bradenton and still catch the flight, and you're too young to keep the rental car. If you can find the keys, you can drive that old beater of your Grandpa's."

Beater? The Riviera?

"I don't need money, Mom. I have my own, from substitute teaching."

Bless that boy.

Stephanie considers this, then returns the bills to her purse. How did I raise such a tight-fisted daughter? Then, just like that, they're gone. I have no idea when and if I'll see Michael again and this worries me. Maybe he didn't understand what I said. Maybe he doesn't care.

No, I decide. I have to believe he understands and cares enough to help.

MAYBE BELIEVING in Michael was a bit premature.

It's after five and I'm still strapped in bed. They've let me up twice, to go to the restroom, but there was no opportunity of another escape. The orderlies are bigger and badder than yesterday. They barely speak, and when they strap me back in bed, they pull the straps tight. It's a terrible existence, made only slightly more tolerable by the pretty little southern girl who returns to feed me my dinner. Her name, I discover, is Wendy, and she's from Murfreesboro, Tennessee. She moved to Florida three months ago to live the dream, but she sadly admits that the dream so far has consisted of a one-room efficiency apartment nine miles from the beach. Wendy tells me all this despite the fact that I am mute during the entire meal. I'm playing up the fake dementia and, so far, I think I'm fooling them. The orderlies, except for Wendy, talk about me as if I'm not even present.

That changes when Dr. Patterson shows up.

"You can't bullshit me, Mr. Flanagan. I know you're hearing and understanding every word I say. Admit it."

I admit nothing. I say nothing.

"We'll be starting a regimen of new medications tomorrow," He continues. "I suspect that the lucid moments will become fewer and further between." He smiles and even winks. "We can't have you running off to Bradenton all the time, can we?"

"Didn't you used to be on TV?" I blurt out. Patterson looks at me curiously.

"No, but I've been told I look like a certain actor. Who are you thinking? Maybe it's the same one."

The ignorant ass has teed it up for me. All I have to do is decide if I want to swing away.

Yeah, I want to swing away.

"I'm sure it was you. Way back in the old times. That horse. The one that talked."

I expect him to become angry, but instead he laughs. He comes closer, still laughing. He leans in to within a few inches of my ear. Then the laughing stops. He becomes dead serious.

"I don't know what type of triumphant comeback you think you've made, old man, but it ends right here." His tone is icy, and I suddenly become worried for my well-being. I'm strapped to a bed in a facility where no one knows me. The two people who can help me are forty miles away, and I have no idea what they've been through since I was hauled away from the park yesterday afternoon. Any hope I have is tied to my twenty-two-year-old grandson, and I'm still not sure he believes I'm lucid enough to make any sense. I realize I should've played it straight from the moment Stephanie walked in. She needed to see the real me, her real father. How hard would it have been for her to walk away had I pleaded with her to get me out? That mistake is already made, but I can stop the charade here and now, and find out if Dr. Patterson has even a bit of remaining conscience.

"You know I'm not suffering from dementia at the moment, Dr. Patterson. You picked up on it yesterday. You described perfectly what I'm experiencing."

Patterson draws back. He gives me an apprising look, as if trying to determine if I'm on the level or not.

"Yeah, Doctor, I walked out of Pinehurst Pavilion and went back to my old home. For the past several days I've been living a somewhat normal life, at least until nightfall."

Patterson nods. "I suspected as much."

"You need to know that I'm not the bad guy in this movie. Trevor Stanley is. He's ruining my old company for his own personal gain. You saw him fire Grady Longacre yesterday. That man has been a loyal employee for thirty years. Trevor has assured himself total control by buying my daughter's favor. But do you want to know the worst, Dr. Patterson?"

Patterson steps away from the bed to close the door. He turns and says, "Tell me the worst, Mr. Flanagan."

"He has a housekeeper, a woman named Sita. He brought her here on false pretenses and forces her to work for him and his family. Her son drowned in Trevor's pool, yet he continues to force her to work."

I can see I've made an impression. Patterson chews on this for a few moments while he stares at the floor. I decide to press on.

"He's a terrible man, Dr. Patterson. He needs to be stopped. He's worried that I'll be the person to do it, so he's made some kind of arrangement with you."

"Yes," Patterson says slowly. "Yes, he has."

"Do you want to be a part of what that man has done? Is that really the kind of doctor you are?"

Patterson doesn't reply, but he appears troubled. He's biting his lip; his eyes remain downcast. I consider pleading my case further but feel like I've given it my best. The rest is up to him. He looks up for a moment. Our eyes meet. He consults the clipboard he's been carrying. He looks at me again. Then he speaks.

"You're my primary concern, Mr. Flanagan. You're my patient, not Mr. Stanley."

Is that a glimmer of hope? I'll not get my hopes up, but maybe it is.

"My decisions regarding your care will be driven by what's best for you."

"I appreciate that, Dr. Patterson."

"How much of the day are you lucid?"

"From the moment I wake up until six in the evening, or thereabouts. A couple days ago I was alert until much later, but I lost the following morning."

And missed an appointment with the FBI, but I'll keep that to myself for now.

He consults my chart again. "I have to tell you, that's practically unheard of. Alzheimer's and dementia patients certainly have periods of lucidity, but they're not that predictable nor prolonged. You just might be some kind of medical miracle, Mr. Flanagan."

"I don't know about that, but what I do know is that I don't need to be strapped down to a hospital bed. I need—I want—to spend time with my friends."

Again, he nods. "I can understand why."

We're making extended eye contact for the first time. I see something that wasn't in those eyes before. He is concerned. He cares. He's considering me as a person rather than a payday.

"Of course, I have concerns," he says. I ask him to share them.

"Last night you left here on your own, a very brave and well-considered escape, I might add."

I say nothing.

"You found your way to an underpass in a very dangerous part of St. Petersburg."

"I did what I had to do. Your facility isn't exactly in the best part of town to start with."

He laughs. "You convinced someone to let you use a telephone, you somehow got ahold of your lady friend... what's her name again?"

"Claire. Claire Tatum."

"You reached Ms. Tatum and told her where to pick

you up."

"Yes."

"What do you remember after that, Mr. Flanagan?"

I'm reluctant to admit that I can't remember much else. I don't know if Claire showed up or if Patterson's people got to me first. The next thing I remember is waking up this morning.

"You don't remember, do you?"

"No."

"Allow me to fill you in. And, Mr. Flanagan, this will be difficult to hear."

I feel myself tense with the realization that something terrible has happened to Claire. Or has it? For all I know Patterson could be lying. Still, I have to hear what he has to say.

"Ms. Tatum arrived at the underpass, but by then you had regressed. She approached the group you were with, but they refused to let you go."

Patterson takes a maddening pause. After a couple deep breaths that could be a reluctance to share difficult information or good impromptu stage acting, he says softly. "Ms. Tatum threatened to call the police, but never got the chance."

"You're lying."

"I wish I was, Mr. Flanagan. They beat her badly. Her car was stolen. She's—"

"You're lying. That did not happen. She would've brought Grady with her."

"Ms. Tatum tried to call him, but he didn't have his phone. He was at his office, where he was supposed to be gathering his belongings." Another deep breath, then, "Grady Longacre killed himself last night at eight-forty."

"That's bullshit!" I strain against the straps. "Grady

didn't even have a gun! That bastard Ballentine took it from him in the park!"

"The gun that belonged to his father? Didn't he tell you he had two?"

I feel as if everything inside me is turned upside down. How would Patterson know about Grady's gun having been his father's? Still, the man is associated with Trevor, and I know Trevor isn't the person I thought he was.

"Lies." I say the word, but don't feel it. Whether it's true or not, I have no way to check. "Did Stephanie know about Grady?"

"Mr. Stanley asked me not to share that information with her. He knew how upset she would be and how in turn she would upset you."

I lie back in bed and try to absorb what Patterson has told me. It just makes no sense. Grady was past the point where he wanted to kill himself, wasn't he? And Claire? Dear, sweet Claire. She wouldn't have walked into an ambush. Or would she? Then, realization hits with the force of a thousand bombs. If she did walk into an ambush, she did it for me. And yes, I know with total certainty that she would do anything for me. The realization is crushing. I find myself starting to drift and silently curse the disease that chomps at my brain like a shark devouring chum.

Claire is hurt. Claire is hurting.

Grady is dead.

And here I am. In a place where I'm unable to get the truth. All I have is what I'm being told by a doctor who I still feel is capable of lying about such terrible things without a second thought.

"How do you know all of this?" I ask as I try to hold on to the moment.

"You were wandering around the area. The police were

investigating Ms. Tatum's assault and came across you. They saw the name of our facility on your gown and called us. Mr. Longacre's death was reported to me by Mr. Stanley."

I'm speechless and starting to drift even more. When he speaks again, Patterson's words seem to be coming from behind a thick curtain. They're muffled and distant, but I can still make them out.

"Had you not tried to escape, Ms. Tatum would be just fine. Her condition is on you."

The words bring oppressive pain to my chest. If it's a heart attack I hope it takes me.

"For your own good, Mr. Flanagan, you need to stay here."

I'm drifting further. Further.

"There's no place else for you to go."

Drifting.

Drifting.

I AWAKEN AND KNOW EXACTLY WHERE I AM.

Same room. Same bed. I'm still strapped in. The window shade in the room where I'm being held is pulled, and the only light is what little comes from a tiny nightlight and the red numerals of a wall clock that flash seven-seventeen AM. My thoughts immediately go to Claire, but before I have time to process my fear that she's alone in some St. Pete hospital, I realize there are three people standing around my bed. I squint in an attempt to make out their faces. Two are men, well dressed in conservative suits with conservative ties and conservative haircuts. They stand on each side of my bed. I look from one to the other, but don't recognize either and wonder if I'm still under Alzheimer's spell. Then I get a good look at the woman at the end of my bed and know I'm not.

"Hello, Mr. Flanagan."

I try to speak, but my throat is dry and all I can manage are a couple of inaudible squeaks. She nods at the man on my right who pours me a cup of water while the other man presses a button that raises my head. The water is placed under my lips and I drink until the cup is empty. I nod my appreciation then return my attention to her. The years I've been locked away inside myself have been kind to her. I do the math and figure she has to be in her early seventies, yet her face and bearing are that of a woman two decades younger. She's tall and slender and she commands the tiny hospital room

"Hello, Director Newsome."

I resist saying more for fear of coming across as frantic, though I am actually very frantic to find out if what Patterson told me about Claire and Grady is true.

FBI Director Gwendolyn Abbott-Newsome offers the slightest of smiles. It disappears quickly, though, and she's all business. "Before we go any further, I need to ask you some questions."

"Yes, ma'am. I have some questions as well. Can you tell me if—"

"If you don't mind, Mr. Flanagan. My questions come first."

"Where is Dr. Patterson?"

A flash of irritation crosses Director Newsome's face. "I'll give you that one," she says crisply. "He's in his office. What happens with him next will depend upon the answers you provide to my questions."

"Yes, ma'am." Without thinking I start to ask about her husband, Byron, since we're friends, but she shuts me down.

"Please tell me your full name."

I do.

"What is your birthdate?"

I tell her.

"What is your wife's name?"

"Her name is Rosalie. But she passed away some time ago."

"What is your daughter's name?"

I provide Stephanie's name and toss in Randy's and Michael's while I'm at it. I tell her where they live and their ages, though I'm fuzzy on Randy's. Is he a year older than Stephanie or a year younger? She seems satisfied.

"What was your previous residence?"

I give her the address on Dolphin Court. "But more recently I was a resident at Pinehurst Pavilion in Bradenton. I was in the unit for Alzheimer's and dementia patients."

"Are you suffering from Alzheimer's?"

"Yes and no." I tell her about waking up and knowing where I was and about how I walked away. I tell her how my mind is clear during the day but fades with the sun. I don't mention Claire or Grady for fear that she'll have news I don't want to hear. Her facial expression hardly changes at all, but when I glance at the men, I see a softening of their features. They're believing me. I have to assume she is, too.

And then she nods at the men again and they remove the restraints. I try to move my arms but can't.

"Give your muscles a couple minutes to start working," the man on my right says as he pats my shoulder. They wait while the feeling returns. "Do you need to use the restroom?" he asks after a couple moments. I do, and he helps me to the door. I close it behind me and do my business. When I return, they are waiting. I crawl back onto the bed but don't lie down. Director Newsome introduces the men as Field Agents Hatcher and Cruz.

"We know you were brought here against your will," Director Newsome says. "When you missed your appointment with Agent Hockenberry at our field office two days ago, these gentlemen began surveilling you at my request."

"Thank you, Director. I wasn't sure you would remember me."

She smiles again, this one seems genuine. "Frankly, Mr. Flanagan, I didn't until Agent Cruz shared your file with me. My husband still uses his Flanagan desk every day. He sends warm wishes. He reminded me that we met once at a dinner party at the home of a Senator from someplace back West."

"Yes, ma'am. Wyoming."

"I must say that the last few shipments of furniture we've purchased have been shoddy. I've removed your company from our vendor list."

"It's junk," I say with more venom than I intend. "Trevor Stanley has ruined the company, but ma'am, I have to ask you a question." I don't wait for her to agree. "Claire Tatum—she's my... friend—and my longtime employee, Grady Longacre... Dr. Patterson said that..." I can't get the words—injured, dead—to cross my lips. "Do you know if they're okay?"

"They are fine."

Her answer brings me to tears. It takes me a spell to pull myself together. Field Agent Hatcher hands me tissues. Agent Cruz pours another cup of water. Director Newsome steps a few feet back, whispers into a cellphone she pulls from her pocket, then returns.

"I thought... he told me Grady was dead."

"Why did you call the FBI, Mr. Flanagan?"

"Trevor Stanley is destroying my company. You've seen the results in the furniture your agency has purchased, Director. He's not the person I thought he—"

"People make bad business decisions all the time, Mr. Flanagan. That's not the dominion of the FBI. You should know that." Her tone leaves no room for argument, so I drop that line.

"Grady Longacre took me to his house. Trevor's house. He has a woman there. She's being held against her will."

The Director's left eye twitches almost imperceptibly, something that wouldn't be noticeable on most people, but on her poker face it changes her entire countenance. The agents pick up on it, too. Cruz starts typing on his cellphone and Hatcher steps closer. What I've just said has caused a shift in the mood of the room, so I elaborate.

"Her name is Sita. She was brought here from Cambodia. She was pregnant when she arrived. Her son died in Trevor's swimming pool this past summer."

"She told you this?" Director Newsome asks.

"I learned most of it from Grady, but I've spoken to Sita, too. Her English isn't great, but I have no doubt after meeting her that she's being held against her will. We— Grady, Claire, and I—wanted to get her out of there, but we didn't get the chance." I pause, my friends still heavy on my mind, and say, "They really are okay? Claire and Grady?"

"Very much so."

I'm happy, but also pissed. "That Dr. Patterson is a snake, Director."

She nods at Hatcher. "Go get him."

After Hatcher leaves, the Director explains what's happening. "Human trafficking from Asia and Mexico is big business, Mr. Flanagan. Whenever there's money to be made, you'll find the usual suspects. Organized crime, cartels, that kind of thing. We have entire divisions of the Bureau dedicated to pursuing and bringing them to justice. It's people like Mr. Stanley, though, who are increasingly becoming a thorn in our side. Small-timers, really. They establish contacts in other countries, begin doing business, then use the relationship to bring people into our country to provide slave labor."

"Do you already know about Trevor?"

"The Bureau knows of him, and he fits the profile for someone who would do this kind of thing. What we didn't have was evidence. That's where you come in."

That's when Agent Hatcher returns. A female is with him, her appearance says loud and clear that she's also from the Bureau. And with them, Dr. Patterson.

"This is Agent Hockenberry, Mr. Flanagan. You spoke to her on the phone when you called a couple days ago."

I say hello. Agent Hockenberry smiles and returns my greeting.

"And," Director Newsome continues, "you already know Dr. Patterson."

Patterson's cocky demeanor has largely disappeared, though I detect some lingering fight in his eyes. He looks at the three agents, then at Director Newsome, and starts to speak. The Director cuts him off.

"I have a plane to catch." She offers her hand to me. "Mr. Flanagan, you're in capable hands with our field agents. I wish you well."

She sweeps out of the room, taking with her an aura that I would expect in the presence of royalty. And once her aura was gone, the local agents waste no time getting down to work.

"Show us Mr. Flanagan's medical charts," Cruz says.

"Are you stupid?" Patterson says testily. "You can't see anything without a search warrant."

Cruz is holding the warrant in Patterson's ugly face before he finishes his sentence. This, I'll admit, is pretty cool. These guys and lady have their act together.

"We are yet to receive Mr. Flanagan's records from the facility in Bradenton."

"Show us what you have, then. You certainly don't have a resident without a file."

Patterson tells them where the files are located. Hatcher goes to get them. Hockenberry and Cruz remain.

"What's your relationship with Trevor Stanley?" Cruz asks in a tone that dares the doctor to object.

"None of your business."

"Dr. Patterson, do you currently have any domestic servants working in your home?"

"None of your business."

Cruz checks his watch. "It's five past eight. How about I send a half-dozen agents to storm your house to find out? Your wife is home, right, Doctor? Phyllis is her name, if I'm not mistaken."

I suspect that Cruz already knows the answer to his question.

"And your two children, Riley and Nala, they're home, too, right?"

This is the closest thing I've ever experienced to one of those TV cop shows in real life. Patterson looks scared when Cruz mentions his family. I thought he might ask to see their search warrant, but he doesn't.

"Susie and Bert. Susie is our housekeeper. Bert takes care of our landscaping and garden."

"And their real names are?"

Patterson shrugs. "I never bothered to learn them."

"What are their home countries?"

"I never bothered to learn them."

Patterson is a real piece of work.

"How did they come to work for you?" Cruz is undeterred.

"I placed ads in the local papers. They answered them."

"How much are they paid?"

"I don't remember. Let me make a call and find out."

"Not necessary. There will be payroll records. There's no way we're letting you near a telephone."

"Are you paying them, Doctor?"

"They make a living wage. My wife and I paid for their travel from their home country. We're paying the fees for them to become United States citizens."

Cruz nods. "How many hours a week do they work?"

"I have no idea."

"We'll go by your house and ask your wife, then."

The family angle works again.

"Phyllis doesn't know. Our accountants take care of that kind of thing."

"Ah, I see. We'll call your accountants, then, assuming you want them dragged into this mess. Is that what you want, Doctor? Do you want your accountants to know about the people in your home?"

"I need to call my lawyer."

"Fair enough," Cruz says as he gets to his feet. "Personal lawyer? Or do you have a separate one for your business?"

"One and the same."

"Feel free to use my phone." Cruz holds out his cell. "Tell him to meet us at the Bureau's Tampa field office. You'll be there until we get the answers we're not getting here."

Patterson hesitates. At the same time Hatcher returns with a skimpy manila file with my name scrawled on the tab.

"One sheet of paper in here," Hatcher says. "Orders for some meds to start today at nine."

"What are the meds?" Cruz asks Patterson.

"I want my lawyer."

"Is Mr. Flanagan suffering from Alzheimer's?" Agent Hockenberry jumps in with the question. Her tone is friendlier and seems to throw Patterson off. He looks at her, then at me.

"He has that or some form of dementia, but he has been experiencing periods of prolonged lucidity."

"These meds," Hockenberry says after glancing at the sheet from my file. "They're sedatives. They'll knock Mr. Flanagan out and keep him out."

"You don't know what you're talking about," Patterson snaps.

"Sure, I do. I was a chemistry major in college."

I wonder what a chem major is doing working as a Federal agent. It's a question that will have to wait. Patterson looks as if he's about to crumble.

"I want my lawyer."

"How about you work with us instead of against us?" Cruz says quickly. "I'll give you fifteen seconds to decide, but remember this: you have two domestic servants working in your home whom we suspect are being held against their will. In about an hour you plan to administer sedatives to an otherwise healthy and alert man. That alone is enough for us to begin crawling all over your practice and your personal life."

"I need to speak to my lawyer first."

"Ten seconds to decide."

"Could I go to jail?"

"Oh, yeah, you're going to prison either way," Cruz replies. "The question is whether or not you ever want to see the outside world again."

"Or which prison you go to," Hatcher adds. "Sheridan, Oregon, is a long way from St. Petersburg, Florida."

"Sumterville's not far, though," Cruz says. "Are you familiar with Sumterville, Doctor?"

Patterson shakes his head.

"Ninety minutes northeast of here. An easy drive for Phyllis and the kids."

Hatcher says, "And just forty-five minutes from Disney World. Riley and Nala are, what, Doc? Twelve and fourteen? They'd probably appreciate a day at Disney after visiting dear old Dad in federal lockup."

Things are suddenly moving faster than Patterson can keep up. I sense he's about to make a life-changing decision. The agents wait quietly while he mulls it over. Agent Cruz still has his phone in his hand, ready if Patterson wants to call his lawyer.

He doesn't.

"Trevor Stanley provided the domestics. They've been with me for nearly a year. I paid an upfront fee."

"And what about Mr. Flanagan?" Cruz asks as he tucks away his phone.

"He was brought here by Trevor Stanley and his people. I was given strict orders that he's never to leave."

THE SIGHT of the old family Christmas tree in the front window of 617 Dolphin Court brings back the warm feelings I've not had in a couple days. It's barely past noon, yet someone, I assume Michael, has seen fit to turn on the tree lights. Grady's car is in the driveway. Claire's is parked on the street. None of them, Michael, Claire, or Grady, know that I'm on my way home. Nor do they know where things stand in regard to the situation with Trevor. That's the way the agents wanted it.

Agent Hockenberry pulls in behind Grady's car then turns to me and smiles brightly.

"Do you think they'll be happy to see you?" she asks.

"As happy as I was to hear they're okay."

She's a good one, Agent Hockenberry. She must've missed the portion of training where they teach poker faces and serious dispositions. Good for her. When Agents Cruz and Hatcher said they were peeling off to work on other things, I was pleased that Agent Hockenberry was escorting me back to Bradenton.

We get out and go up onto the porch. This was my house for decades, yet for some reason I feel the need to ring the doorbell. I'm glad I do. Michael answers and pulls me into a fierce hug. Over his shoulder I see Grady and Claire. I'm as elated as I've ever been in my life. Grady takes his turn with the hugging, then I go to Claire. The kiss we exchange would've earned a PG-13 at the movie theater a few years ago. I don't care. I love this woman more than anyone or anything I've ever loved. The ache I felt when Patterson was spewing his lies about her is a distant memory as I hold this beautiful woman in my arms. Then, behind me I hear someone clear her throat.

Agent Hockenberry. But she's grinning, so I know I'm okay.

"Get a room, you guys," she jokes. "But, please, wait until later, because we have work to do."

We gather in the living room. I take the seat in the center of the sofa. Claire is on one side of me, Agent Hockenberry on the other. Grady takes my usual spot, a worn leather armchair that Rosalie and I bought on our tenth anniversary. Michael sits on the floor.

And speaking of Michael.

"Your grandson contacted us," Agent Hockenberry said.

"After I talked to Mr. Longacre and Miss Tatum," Michael said sheepishly.

"I wasn't sure if you believed I was coherent or just talking out of my head."

"Something told me you were really you, Grandpa. Then, when I came down to Bradenton I got ahold of Mr. Longacre. He filled me in and I called Agent Hockenberry."

"Patterson told me you were dead," I say to my friend.

"Unemployed, but not dead," Grady said. Then, turning to Agent Hockenberry, he said, "Can we get that bastard, Trevor Stanley?"

"That's our goal, Mr. Longacre. But I need your help."

I feel a lot of different things as Agent Hockenberry explains what needs to happen. Fear isn't the least of those feelings. There's also joy and, more than anything else, exhilaration.

We're going to be helping Sita escape from Trevor's home.

"We don't have probable cause to go barging in, but we feel she'll let you and Grady in," the agent says. "Once you're inside, you'll insist she come with you. When you're off of Stanley's property we can step in for the handoff."

"Say the word," Grady says excitedly.

"Tonight. We'll wait until eight. Mr. Stanley is catching a flight back to his family's vacation spot at six, so he'll be long gone."

"That won't work," I say.

I explain to the agent how my condition worsens in the evening. She considers this for a moment, then excuses herself to step outside and make a phone call. We visit while she's gone. Grady and Claire want to know what I went through, and I tell them. I'm just wrapping up my account when Hockenberry returns.

"You move in at three o'clock. Mr. Longacre. Mr. Flanagan will go with you."

"Will it be safe?" Grady asks. "Trevor's back in town, and his man, Ballentine, tends to check in during the week."

"Our people are monitoring both men. Mr. Stanley has been in his office since seven-fifty this morning. His family is still out of the country on vacation. Ballentine's in Tampa on business. He left Bradenton at ten-fifteen. When he comes out of his meeting, he'll be dismayed to find that his car has been towed. It will take him until at least four to get it out of impound."

We laugh at Ballentine's unlucky turn of events.

"It still might be difficult," Hockenberry continues. "After you were there the other day, Sita might've been warned never to open the gate again. Fortunately, we have this." She reaches into her purse and pulls out what looks to be a garage door remote. "It's set on the local emergency frequency. You'll be able to pull through the gates like you own the place." She hands me the remote. "Beyond that, you're on your own."

I'm pumped by what we're about to do. I can see Grady is, too. For a couple of older guys, it promises to be a pretty exciting day. We quickly find out that Hockenberry isn't done yet.

"Mr. Longacre, do you have access to company records?"

"Only a few, but I'm sure Trevor has had me shut off by now."

"Maybe not. Do you have a work-issued laptop?"

Grady seems startled by the question. "Yeah, but I never used it much, other than some work at the end of the fiscal year. It's in my desk drawer at home."

"Can we access it?"

"Sure, but Agent Hockenberry, you'll quickly find that I have no access to anything within the company other than my little repair division. The security people shut me out a long time ago."

"Unfortunately, just as with rescuing the domestic at Mr. Stanley's home, our hands are tied in regard to digging into the Flanagan Furniture information system. We could get a warrant, but it would alert the very people we don't want to be alerted." Hockenberry turns to Michael and says, "But this young man is quite gifted in computer systems and hacking, aren't you, Michael?"

Michael's expression is blank. Hockenberry gives him a wink.

"C'mon, Michael. We're the FBI. We do our homework. We know about your friends..." she opens a binder and checks something. "Harley Christopher and Lora Lynn Bechtel."

The blank expression disappears. Michael seems frightened by what he's hearing. "Really, Agent," he says, his voice quavering, "We've never done anything that—"

"You changed Miss Bechtel's Sociology grade from a C to a B, Michael. I imagine you and Mr. Christopher were too scared about being caught to change it to an A."

Michael nods. "I couldn't sleep for days."

Hockenberry laughs at this. Then, to me she says, "Your grandson knows his way around computers, Mr. Flanagan. He might've hacked into a few places he shouldn't have, but his intentions weren't malicious. If it's okay with all of you, we'll retrieve Mr. Longacre's laptop and see what Michael can find by digging around in the company's system."

It's obvious that Michael is excited about helping. Hockenberry makes another call while I get ready to leave with Grady. It's going to be a wild afternoon, and I feel like a kid at Christmas.

BEACH TRAFFIC IS KNOTTIER than heck, and it's taking us longer to get to Trevor's place on Longboat Key than we'd expected. My excitement ninety minutes ago has dissolved into nervousness. Sure, I was unaware of my surroundings just a week ago, and I guess some would say I'm operating on borrowed time, but still I don't want to meet my demise while trying to gain access to Trevor Stanley's beachfront mini mansion. How much clarity I have remaining is unknown, but regardless of whether it's four hours or four years, I want to spend it with Claire. Michael and Grady, too, but mainly Claire. She's worried about me. She said as much as we were leaving. I promised we would return safe and sound, and it's a promise I want to keep. Christmas is a week away, and if I can have nothing else, I want to spend Christmas day with my forever love.

Grady pulls up to the gate that leads to Trevor's house. I take the remote from my pocket and push the button.

"Works like a charm," Grady says with a breeziness that I bet doesn't match the roiling he's feeling in his stomach. He has to be feeling it. I know I am.

"Pull up to the door," I say. "We'll act like we belong here." He does, then blows the horn three short blasts.

"Maybe she'll just come out," he says. We wait for several minutes, but there's no Sita, so we get out and go around back. There's a wrought iron fence that separates us from the swimming pool and Trevor's manicured back lawn. It's more ornamental than useful, with iron spindles spaced about eight inches apart and a height that I estimate to be six feet. We walk to the gate and try it, but it's locked. I survey the fence for another entry point. Grady does the same. There's none. Now we're eyeing the entire length. I would bet the mortgage that Grady's thinking the same thing I am.

"I can't," I say.

"Me neither," Grady answers. "Maybe twenty years ago, but my fat ass ain't going over anymore."

"I could lift you up," I suggest.

Grady snorts. "And what's going to break my fall on the other side?"

He has a point.

"How about I lift you up," he counters.

I take another look around, just to make sure no one is watching what is quickly becoming a scene out of a Laurel and Hardy movie. It's just us, so I eye the fence one more time, then say, "Cup your hands down low. I'll step in them and you can lift me up."

"Then what?"

"I fall on the other side, probably break a hip. Do you know the address?"

"No, why?"

"You'll need it when you call the ambulance."

We dissolve into a giggling fit that defies the situation. Grady is laughing so hard he's leaning against the fence to catch his breath. Then he farts and that makes us laugh harder.

"Can you believe," he says between gasps, "the freaking Federal Bureau of Investigation sent us old bastards out here to rescue someone? We can't even get over the damned fence."

I can't stop giggling like a little girl. "Those guys are in charge of protecting our country from the bad guys, and we're the best they can do."

We remain like that for a spell, tittering, rechecking the fence to see if it's magically become smaller, then giggling some more. Soon enough, though, the merriment starts to ebb away, replaced by the realization that we've been sent here with a job to do and, so far, we've fallen well short.

"Okay," I finally say. "Lift me up."

I hear bones creaking as Grady bends low. He emits another fart, but we're past laughing now. I place my left foot in his hands, and he hoists me upward. When my thighs reach the top of the fence, I grab it and try to hurtle over it sideways. My foot catches and I stumble. Suddenly I'm falling headfirst. Fortunately, I still have both hands on the fence. I use them to slow my descent and turn just enough to absorb the impact with my right shoulder. I'm expecting a separated shoulder but feel nothing. Did I really fall? Yeah, I did. What I hadn't planned was for the grass on the other side to be so lush, more like falling into a soft bed than hard ground.

"They must water the lawn a lot," I observe. I look up and see Grady peering at me through the fence, as if he's in a jail cell. I motion to the gate, get up, and head that way. He follows. It opens easily from my side, and I let him in.

"That's where she lives," he says, nodding at a small structure I had assumed was a changing room. The reality of why we're here hits me hard. The pool in front of us is where Sita's little boy, Narith, lost his life. It didn't have to happen, I remind myself. Trevor Stanley could've given Sita a few moments to tuck him back inside their little living quarters. Narith's death is on Trevor Stanley, and I feel something akin to pure hatred washing over me, pushing aside any lingering doubts as to why we're here.

We approach the tiny structure and knock.

"Sita?" Grady calls out. There is no reply. I peer through a window into a single room with two small beds, a microwave oven, and a threadbare armchair. No television, no sofa, no refrigerator.

"That bastard," I say aloud. I turn to Grady and say, "She must be in the house."

As we pass the pool neither of us says what's on our minds. I'm trying not to imagine a little boy, a precious child, tumbling to his death in the waters a few feet away. Grady's probably thinking of little Narith as well.

We knock on the back door. No one comes. We knock louder. Still nothing.

"Do you think he took her away?" I ask.

"If Trevor suspected for a moment that the FBI was on to him, you bet your ass he did." Grady scratches his chin. "But I don't think he knows, so let's go on in."

Grady picks up a flowerpot on the edge of the back patio and chucks it with everything he has at a window next to the door. It bounces off and breaks into a million pieces when it falls to the concrete a few feet away.

"I guess your arm's not what it used to be, Grady."

"I need something bigger." While Grady surveys the patio for a larger flowerpot I try turning the doorknob. It works. I push the door open.

"Grady," I say to get his attention. He turns, sees what I've done, and swears at himself for not trying it first.

"I'll have a sore arm tomorrow, and for what?" he muses as he follows me inside.

"Sita?" I call out. "It's Neal Flanagan and your friend, Grady Longacre."

"Hello, Sita?"

Nothing.

We step further inside, through the small entry way into the kitchen where we visited with Sita a few days earlier. Still no sign of her.

"She doesn't have a car, so if she's gone, she had to go with someone," Grady says.

Then, we both hear something. Just a small sound, like fingers rubbing across a hard surface, almost a sweeping sound. Grady is looking around, trying to determine where it came from. I have already figured it out. I approach a tall cabinet in the corner of the kitchen and pull it open.

"Sita, it's okay. We're not going to hurt you. We've come to rescue you."

Sita dissolves into tears. It's as if she wants to believe me, but either can't or won't. Grady joins me. Sita has had to squeeze herself tightly to fit into the small space. I offer my hand, but she cowers and shakes her head.

"You're safe, Sita," Grady says. "Trevor won't hurt you anymore. We're taking you away."

When she speaks it comes out as a torrent of words in a language we don't know. Her tone is frantic. Her eyes are hooded by fear. I have no idea what to say, but Grady seems to have intuited something.

"Did he tell you not to let us in?"

Sita nods.

"Did he tell you we are bad?"

Again, she nods.

"Sita, you know I'm not bad. Do not believe what Trevor told you. We said we would save you, and we are here to do it."

I'm not sure Sita understands everything Grady says, but she can tell from the way he says it that we're not going to harm her. She slowly steps out of the closet. We move back a few steps to avoid crowding her.

"You are going with us. You will be safe," Grady says. This time Sita nods.

"Do you want to get your things?" I ask. Sita doesn't understand, so we lead her back to her tiny living quarters. Grady points at her few items of clothes hung on hooks in a corner.

"Do you want to take these?"

Sita backs away from them and I understand why. What is hanging on the hooks are several versions of the same thing: a domestic's uniform. I glance around and see that Sita has no other clothing. She goes to one of the tiny beds, lifts the mattress, and removes an envelope. We don't ask what's inside and she doesn't tell us.

"Are you ready to leave?" Grady asks, pointing to the door.

She is. And we do.

It's getting to where I can start to feel the fade. I noticed it for the first time at Patterson's facility, and again tonight. A slight headache is the initial signal that, like Cinderella at the stroke of midnight, I'm soon going to be checking out.

We arrive at my house at ten before six getting stuck in the rush of tourists leaving Anna Maria Island after sundown. Agent Hockenberry greets us on my front porch. Grady whispers something to her, then I see both of them look my way.

"Yep," I say softly. "It's happening."

Grady returns to the car to help Sita understand that she's safe. Hockenberry takes me inside. Claire greets me just inside the door, gives me a big kiss, and says, "If you'll excuse us, I'll take him upstairs." I like the sound of that.

"Did Michael find anything?" I ask as she's helping me get undressed.

"Michael found plenty," she coos. "But we can talk about that tomorrow." She hugs me tightly, looks into my eyes, and says, "I love you, Neal."

"I love you too, sweetheart. Let's get married."

CHAPTER TWELVE
SATURDAY, DECEMBER 19

I AWAKEN AND KNOW EXACTLY WHERE I AM.

Claire isn't next to me, but there is a Hawaiian-themed pair of men's swim trunks on a clothes hanger hooked over the bedroom door. They're pale blue and white and yellow and have pink flamingos all over them. Certainly not the kind of thing I would've ever worn in the past, but I sense that's about to change.

"I hear you moving around in there," Claire calls from the hallway bathroom. "Let's go swimming."

I do as I'm told, throwing off the sheets, getting out of bed, and slipping on the flamingos. I look at myself in the mirror and laugh. The suit swallows me up, making my legs look like pale matchsticks. Claire comes back in while I'm admiring myself. She sidles up behind me, and I catch a glimpse of her in the mirror and can't believe how lovely she is. Her swimsuit is a white one-piece, modest, yet incredibly sexy.

"Wow." I say it and mean it. She smiles, kisses me softly on the cheek, and runs her fingers down my back in a way that gives me chills. We remain that way for several moments while my mind wanders. I think back to yesterday. Fragments form into complete memories.

Waking up in Patterson's hellish facility.

The appearance of FBI Director Newsome and her people.

Their takedown of Patterson.

Coming home to Claire, Grady, and Michael.

Sita's rescue.

And the last thing I remember, oh my goodness.

"I kinda asked you to marry me last night." I say as I take a seat on the bed.

Claire giggles as she sits down next to me.

"Kinda?"

"Maybe more than kinda?"

"You really remember that?"

I nod.

"I'm surprised, because by the time you said that you'd already started to fade away."

"What I don't remember is your answer."

"That's because I didn't give you one. Two minutes later you started talking about how Grady needed to go see the people who run the Diplomat Hotel in Philadelphia, something about a special order."

"Did you mean it?"

"Of course. Grady was the only person I trusted to get those measurements."

Claire hits me playfully. "Don't toy with a girl's heart, Neal Flanagan."

I take her hand and turn so we're facing each other. I want her to know that the words I'm about to say come from my heart.

"I would love nothing more than to be married to you, Claire."

She doesn't say anything, and I suspect she's having the same concerns I am.

"If life were a storybook, we would get married today," I say after a few moments.

Claire gets to her feet. "Right this moment, darling, life is better than a storybook. Let's go swimming."

We're on our way downstairs when I think to ask what Michael discovered while trying to get into the Flanagan computer system.

"Enough, it appears. The main system proved too hard to crack, but Grady's little corner of the system contained payroll files for people who don't really work there."

"Grady mentioned something about that."

"Agent Hockenberry ran the names through the FBI's database. They're all fake."

"Where does that leave us?"

"Agent Hockenberry is continuing to work on things. They took Sita to a safe house last night. That was the last I heard."

A thought comes to me, one that could jeopardize everything. "Trevor had to find out that Sita was gone when he went home last evening. What did they do about that?"

"He didn't go home. He went straight to the airport to catch a flight back to his family's vacation place in Asia."

"How about Ballentine?"

"That story only gets better. When he went to pick up his car the Hillsborough County PD found there were arrest warrants on him in Miami and Charlotte, North Carolina. He's getting a tour of the southeast United States as we speak. Miami first, then Charlotte. He's going to be out of the way at least through Christmas."

With this piece of good news Claire and I head to the

pool. She informs me that Michael left an hour ago to meet up with Grady. I wonder what they're plotting, but don't care enough to call and find out. It's just me and my girl, sunshine, and the pool. I'm going to milk the moment for all it's worth.

We're relaxing poolside when Grady and Michael show up with Agent Hockenberry. They pull up chairs and surround us. Grady speaks first.

"Neal, it's time for you to take back your role as President of Flanagan Furniture."

I don't know what to say, but it seems the three of them have things all figured out. Grady defers to Agent Hockenberry.

"We have an appointment in federal court in Tampa on Monday. We're going to get your daughter's power of attorney overturned."

I can hardly believe what I'm hearing.

"They'll fight it. Trevor for sure. Probably Stephanie and Randy, too. There's plenty of evidence that I'm suffering from dementia."

"You'll be right there in court to refute that evidence," Hockenberry explains. "And if that's not enough, we have some other tricks up our sleeves."

"What about Trevor?" I ask. "He's on the other side of the world."

"I suspect he'll be getting word any time now about the hearing. I would anticipate his return in time to be there. Your daughter and son-in-law have already booked flights to Tampa for tomorrow afternoon."

I look at Michael. The last thing I want is for him to be

stuck in the middle of things. "What do you think of this?" I ask.

"When we used to visit you as a kid, I would tell Mom and Dad that I wanted to work with Grandpa at the furniture factory," he says. "Maybe I'll still have that chance."

I'm touched, but also concerned. "You realize this will go against your parents' wishes, don't you, Michael?"

"I've seen enough of what Trevor Stanley is doing to realize that Mom placed her trust in the wrong person. She should've been supporting you all along, Grandpa."

I glance at Claire and almost wish she wasn't seated next to me. The next question I need to ask my grandson could hurt her.

"Do you know why your mother sided against me?"

Michael lowers his head for a moment, then looks up at Claire and offers her a warm smile. "She holds a grudge over stuff that happened a long time ago. That stuff can't be changed, but family is family. Mom should've been there for you more since you went to live at the nursing home. That's on her."

It's quiet while we absorb what Michael has just said. The boy is proving to be wise beyond his years, and I'm suddenly excited for the chance to regain control of my company, even if only to right some wrongs before turning it over to him someday.

"Of course, Trevor will still retain a thirty percent share of the company," Grady reminds us.

"I guess we just have to deal with that," I say.

We spend the next few minutes discussing the formalities of our court appearance. Agent Hockenberry seems to have taken every possible scenario into consideration, so I feel comfortable. When she gets up to leave, Grady and Michael do the same.

"I'm staying with Mr. Longacre until the hearing," Michael announces. "Grandpa, you and Ms. Tatum can have the place to yourselves."

I consider raising a protest, but Claire squeezes my hand. "Don't you worry about us," she says happily. "We'll have a mini-vacation right here by the swimming pool."

OUR FIRST STOP is a shiny new shopping mall in Sarasota. It, like a lot of things out by the interstate, wasn't here before. We're here to Christmas shop, but it's lunchtime so Claire recommends a sit-down place just inside the mall's main entrance. We're seated and given menus.

"Claire, something's been bothering me."

She looks at me over the top of a menu large enough to square dance on.

"You're putting out a lot of money for me."

This makes her smile, but I press on. The room where we stayed at the Ritz was comped by a long-time customer of the company, but I've seen where Claire lives. She probably doesn't have the kind of money needed for restaurant lunches and Christmas presents.

"I have a little saved up," she says. "What better to spend it on than you and me."

"I appreciate that, but after I'm... wherever I go... if I go... I don't want you to be short on money for the things you need."

The server comes and we order. A burger for me, some kind of salad in an edible bowl for Claire. While we wait for our food, we decide to Christmas shop without really buying anything. "Show me what you would buy me if you could," she says. "And I'll do the same."

The burger is huge and delicious, and the shopping is fun. Claire runs into several people she knows, and she's always quick to introduce me as her special friend. That's the way older folks keep from using terms younger people use, like boyfriend or lover. I like the way it sounds and hope I might see someone I used to know so I can try it out. Unfortunately, that doesn't happen, but it's the only disappointment in an otherwise wonderful day. We walk the mall from one end to the other, up, down, around, and back again. We peer in windows and browse through stacks and racks. Claire tries on a dress that is the same color as her eyes. It looks magnificent on her, and I tell her so. My words make her gush with happiness. If it weren't for the frequent mirrors we pass that remind me of my age, I could forget that I'm not in my teens or twenties, experiencing real love for the first time all over again.

We stop at an ice cream stand for waffle cones, and I notice the crowds of shoppers that I'd scarcely taken note of before. Several young couples sit around us, enjoying ice cream cones and conversation. I subtly check out the women in these couples and am certain that mine is the prettiest. I tell her this and she blushes.

"I've had enough shopping," she says between licks of strawberry ice cream.

"What would you like to do next?"

She nods toward the mall exit. "I think you can guess."

She takes my hand, and I fall for her all over again.

"I'm famished," I say as we make our way downstairs.

"Romance will do that to a guy," Claire teases as she leads the way into the kitchen. We check what's in the fridge, then decide to order pizza. Pepperoni is a given. Claire wants hamburger, I don't. I want green peppers, she turns her nose up at that. She counters with ham, I say no.

"Onions?"

"No way," she says quickly. "I want minty fresh breath."

We settle on double pepperoni. Joey D's, a local place, says they'll have it to us in forty minutes.

"Maybe *Gulf Coast Gables* offers a good movie channel," I say, poking fun at the ridiculous name my daughter has bestowed on the place. "The *Meyerhoff Family from Drexel Hill, Pennsylvania*, will probably want to watch a movie or two when they get here next week."

I fumble with the TV remote for a few minutes before Claire takes over. She flips through channels but comes up empty. A few more clicks and she squeals with delight.

"*Gulf Coast Gables* has Netflix!"

I have no idea what that is, so she explains as she pulls up a selection of Holiday movies. Some I remember, most not. I never was much of a Christmas movie guy, so I ask her to choose. She narrows it down to *National Lampoon's Christmas Vacation* and *It's a Wonderful Life*. I've seen both. I love both. In the end she settles on *It's a Wonderful Life*. We agree to wait until after the pizza arrives before starting the movie.

We get situated comfortably close on the sofa. I hold her hand.

"Has it been?" I ask, nodding at the movie title frozen on the TV screen.

"A wonderful life?" She thinks on it. "There have been plenty of wonderful moments," she pauses, shrugs, then says, "A person can't spend their life wondering what if."

"Tell me about your life after us." I've steered away from that topic, preferring to focus on the now. But I want to know. If it was difficult, how difficult? She's told me a few things, but I want to hear it all. I can see that she's reluctant, but I gently push her to speak.

Claire's tone is measured as she tells me about the series of jobs she's held over the past decade. Library assistant, teacher's assistant, a stint as a travel agent. "They paid the bills, but there was never much left at the end of the month."

"But you're not working now?"

"I fill in at the library a few days a month, but I started collecting social security last spring, so I don't have to work full time anymore."

Then, out of the blue, she surprises me. "Arch asked me to remarry him."

"Whoa."

"Six years ago. He had remarried, but it didn't work. Nice girl, Martina's her name. She's twenty years younger than me, young enough to know better than to put up with his dark side."

"What happened?"

"Arch slapped her twice. The first time she warned him to never do it again. The second time she divorced him and got the house across the street."

I instinctively look across the living room toward the windows where I can see Claire's former home.

"She sold it pretty quick. That's been a few years ago now. Anyway, Arch kept close tabs on me. He knew I was barely getting by. One day he called and asked for a meeting. I assumed it had something to do with the kids, but he surprised me. He said that he had changed and wanted to forgive and forget."

"Wow."

"Yep," Claire nods. "He was willing to look past my past

indiscretions – that's what he called you and me – and try again."

"What did you think of that?"

"Honestly, Neal, I actually considered saying yes."

I'm surprised, but I'm not. The thought of no longer being financially strapped had to be alluring. Still, knowing how Archie Tatum used to be with his kids and Claire, the mental and physical abuse, I shudder at the thought of Claire returning to that situation.

"I wanted to believe he could change, so I said I would think about it. He was gracious about me considering it, then I ran into Martina, and she told me what he'd done to her." Claire takes a deep breath, smiles sadly, then says, "He hadn't changed, not really. I went to his new house the next morning and told him there was no way I would ever be married to him again."

"Good for you!" I hug her, proud of her bravery and willingness to stand up against the bully Arch Tatum.

"Yes," Claire says, shaking her head. "Six months later Arch married a schoolteacher from up in Sun City Center. They lasted less than a year."

"Where is he now?"

Claire shrugs. "We never talk, and I make it a point never to ask the kids. They don't see much of him either, really. I think he lives on St. Pete Beach, but that's just what I've heard through the grapevine."

There's more I want to know, questions I want to ask, but the pizza arrives. We get plates from the kitchen, a couple bottles of water, and sit back to enjoy pizza and a movie. It's five-fifteen, though, and I'm not sure how much of the movie I'll really see.

But the pizza is certainly good.

CHAPTER THIRTEEN
SUNDAY, DECEMBER 20

I awaken and know exactly where I am.

Claire is snoring softly next to me. I get up quietly and head to the bathroom, then downstairs. There's no coffee, so I decide to go get some. It'll be the first time I've driven since the day I escaped from Pinehurst. I throw on yesterday's clothes and head for the garage. My Riviera is parked where it always is. The keys are in the ignition, a reminder that Michael has probably driven it a time or two. I start it, back out, and drive toward Publix. On the way I pass a place called Starbucks. These little coffee houses are everywhere, though I scarcely remember seeing them when I was here before. I pull into the parking lot and step inside. The place is busy for Sunday morning. I get in line and check the menu while I wait my turn.

A young lady named Daphne greets me warmly. I tell her it's my first time in, and she seems surprised.

"What can I make for you?"

"Just two coffees."

Daphne seems disappointed. "It's your first time here and you order plain coffee?"

I laugh. "Maybe you can recommend something different."

"Certainly. You're ordering for yourself and someone else, right?"

"Yes."

"Tell me about the person you're ordering for."

"She's a little younger than me. Beautiful, with blue eyes and the most wonderful smile you'll ever see."

"I can see she's pretty special to you," Daphne says.

"I asked her to marry me two days ago."

"Did she accept?"

I shake my head. "There are some extenuating circumstances, but it doesn't change the way we feel about each other."

"If that's the case, you need to get her a white chocolate mocha Frappuccino."

I have no idea what she's just said but press on. "And for me?"

"A caramel ribbon crunch Frappuccino."

"Okay, then."

Daphne makes up my drinks, then calls me back to the counter.

"Take these home, hand this one to your friend, and ask her again to marry you."

"You don't understand, Daphne. As I said, there are some things that might get in the way."

"I saw your face when you were describing her," Daphne says as she hands me the drinks. "Nothing should get in the way of what you feel for each other."

CLAIRE MEETS me at the back door. She appears panicked.

"I've called Grady and Michael. I was about to call Agent Hockenberry. I was scared that you'd gotten lost, that perhaps you were..."

She doesn't finish her sentence, but I get her drift. Alzheimer's patients are sometimes known to wander away. She probably woke up, saw I was gone, and was frightened that I hadn't found my daily dose of clarity.

"I'm good. We needed coffee."

I hold up the Starbucks cups as evidence and, if needed, a peace offering. She looks from them to me, then laughs.

"I love Starbucks. What did you get me?"

"This," I say holding out her drink. "I can't remember what it's called, and that's not because I'm having memory issues. Those names they give drinks are long."

She accepts it gratefully and takes a sip. "It's a white chocolate mocha Frappuccino! My favorite. How did you know?"

I tell her about my discussion with Daphne. She finds it uproariously funny that I shared so much personal stuff.

"Know what she told me to do?"

"I have no idea."

"I'm supposed to come home, give you your coffee, and ask you to marry me again."

"You told her you proposed?"

I nod. "She was a very engaging young woman."

"Wow." Claire sips her drink. "Just wow. You really laid it out there for her, didn't you?"

"Do you want me to get down on my knee here or in the living room?"

Claire kisses me. Then kisses me again. "Let's see how tomorrow goes in court first, then take it from there."

"How's that going to change anything?"

"Let's just wait, okay? I have something else I want you to do with me."

I wiggle my eyebrows in a way that I hope comes across as lascivious, but most likely just looks silly. "What would that be?"

"It's almost Christmas, Neal. I want to go to church."

I GREW up going to a Methodist church. Dad was Baptist and Mom was a holy roller from a little cracker town north of the Everglades. They'd argued back and forth before deciding to split the difference. They were never happy with the choice. Dad thought it was an abomination that our church sprinkled water over infants' heads. "You need to be dunked for it to take," he would say every time another young couple brought their infant forward. Mom struggled with how no one spoke in tongues or raised their hands to worship. "Don't they feel *anything*?" she would lament after another somber Sunday. By the time I was seven, they'd stopped going altogether.

Rosalie grew up Lutheran but stopped going the week after she graduated from high school. We were married in that same Lutheran church by a pastor who grumbled nonstop about how it didn't seem right that we didn't attend regularly. As best as I recall, other than weddings and funerals, we never stepped foot in church after that.

But since I will do anything in the world for Claire, I put on a seersucker and my Goodwill shoes and prepare to go to church.

"Arch and I were Catholic," she explains as she drives. "When we split up, he got to keep the church, so we're going to try some place different, a place I pass by from time to time."

The place is called Rock and Redeemer Church. It's tucked in behind a Wawa gas station just off the Tamiami Trail.

"Didn't this used to be an Episcopal Church?" I ask as we enter the parking lot.

"Way back. They built a new place out in Lakewood Ranch fifteen years or so ago. This church was empty for a few years before these people bought it. It's lovely, don't you think?"

It is lovely, especially if you can look past the gas pumps and constant stream of cars pulling in and out of the Wawa. It's smaller than some houses, white, with a bell tower over the front door. There aren't more than fifteen or twenty cars in the parking lot and judging by the way people greet each other as they approach the entrance, everyone knows everyone else.

"We'll stick out like sore thumbs," I observe as we follow them in.

There are only eight rows on each side, each with room for six or eight people. The place would be overflowing with a hundred people. I estimate there to be half that. We're greeted by a happy-looking old man with a name tag that reads, *Hello! My Name is Owen!* He asks our names, and we tell him, then he directs us to seats in the second row. I prefer to be further in the back, though, so we scoot past *Hello! My Name is Owen!* and sit in the third row from the rear. People turn to gawk at us, most offering smiles and season's greetings. A large Christmas tree fills the front of the church, leaving just enough room for a pulpit.

"They're so nice, aren't they?" Claire says as she holds my hand.

At ten-thirty on the nose a skinny guy in a white shirt and too-short tie stands at the pulpit and welcomes everyone. When he asks if there are any guests, all eyes turn to us. After a few uncomfortable moments I rise and say, "My name is Neal, and this is Claire." The skinny guy welcomes us and says they have a gift for us. *Hello! My Name is Owen!* comes up behind us, taps me on the shoulder, and presents us with a box of chocolate candy and a bookmark with the church's image on it.

"We hope y'all come back," the skinny guy says. With that awkward moment behind us, we grab hymnals and join in while the congregation sings Christmas hymns. Claire is right. It is kind of nice.

Following hymns and passing the collection plate, the skinny guy takes a seat and is replaced by a midget. I do a double take. He's been seated in the front row, blocked from my line of sight by an enormous woman in the row ahead of us who keeps popping Smith Brothers cough drops into her mouth during the singing. I glance at Claire and find her glancing at me. "Is he really a midget?" I whisper. The lady in front of me, the cough-drop popper, turns and whispers, "It's not polite to say midget. Pastor Lonnie's a dwarf or a little person. And a mighty man of God."

"I'm sorry," I say, then to Claire, "I had no idea."

"You've been gone awhile," she whispers in reply. "You get a pass this time."

He introduces himself as Pastor Lonnie, and his speaking voice has a deep rich baritone. He stands on a platform behind the pulpit that the skinny guy wheeled into place before sitting down. Pastor Lonnie looks over the heads of his regular attendees, around the cough drop lady, and addresses Claire and me.

"It's good to have you here. We're blessed by your presence." He pauses, then adds, "If you have any questions, see me after the service. I'm known for my short sermons."

Short sermons. For some reason Claire finds this to be the funniest thing she's ever heard. A short man giving short sermons. She laughs hard and loud, then notices no one else is laughing along. Her face grows crimson, and she tries to cover up for herself by starting to cough. The lady in front of us holds out her box of Smith Brothers. Claire takes one.

"Want to make a run for the door?" I whisper.

She hits my arm and refuses to look up. It doesn't take long for Pastor Lonnie to kick into high gear. He preaches with a fervor and intensity that I never saw in our Methodist church, quoting Scripture as flawlessly as some might say their own name. People sitting around us flip through their Bibles trying to keep up, but most are no match for the mighty man of God. A few minutes in, Claire hands me a Bible from the rack in front of us. I open it as Pastor Lonnie directs us to the Book of Luke, but by the time I find Luke in the table of contents Pastor Lonnie has already moved on to Philippians. I set it aside, preferring to listen to his gifted oration.

The hour passes in what seems like seconds, and before I know it, we are heading down the aisle toward the back door. A dozen people thank us for coming and say they hope we'll return. *Hello! My Name is Owen!* slips me his telephone number and encourages us to call if we have questions about the church. When we reach the exit, Pastor Lonnie is waiting for us. He shakes my hand warmly and does the same to Claire.

"This is my wife, Marilyn, and our boys, Ben and Adam," he says motioning to the woman next to him. We say our hellos, thank him for his hospitality, and scurry off to Claire's car.

"What did you think?" she asks once we've pulled past the Wawa onto Tamiami.

"I never considered that a dwarf, or little person, or whatever I'm supposed to call him, might have a regular-sized wife and kids."

She looks at me in disbelief. "That's all you got from today?"

"No," I assure her as I reach for her hand. "They are a very friendly group, aren't they?"

She agrees. "I think I would like to go back."

"Easter is in the spring."

"No, I mean next week. Maybe every week. I felt like I belonged there."

"You certainly made yourself known," I kid. "The way you started laughing."

Her face flushes again. "That was terrible of me. When Pastor Lonnie said he keeps his sermons short, all I could think of was that his sermons are short because he is short."

"Tell you what," I say as we drive north on Tamiami. "If I'm around to go, I'll go back with you."

"You will!" Claire seems genuinely thrilled with what I've said, and that thrills me.

"In fact," I continue, "will you turn around and go back now?"

"Are you serious?" She turns on the turn signal and gets in the right lane. "Do you want to visit with Pastor Lonnie?"

"No," I say, offering her a wink. "I'm craving a fountain drink from Wawa."

WE'RE JUST COMING in from swimming when the house phone rings. I answer and hear Michael's voice.

"Mom and Dad are on their way to town. Is it okay if I come over there to meet them?"

"Of course. Is it okay if I leave you with them? Claire and I will go spend the night at her place. I don't want them to see me when I start to sundown."

A half-hour later we're pulling away from my house. Grady calls on Claire's cell to let us know that he'll pick us up at nine in the morning for the ride to Tampa.

"Are you nervous?" Claire asks after we get off the phone.

"I was, but in the pool earlier I took Pastor Lonnie's advice and prayed."

Claire sets up straighter behind the wheel. "Really?"

"Um-hmm."

"What was that like?"

I shrug. "I can't say, really. I just know that I was worried this morning and now I'm not worried at all."

"From your mouth to God's ears," she says. "What do you want for dinner?"

I look across at her and marvel at how lovely she is. The late afternoon sun is dipping in through her window, casting the right side of her face in delicate shadow. Maybe it's just seeing her next to me, or maybe it's the fact that I prayed today for what might be the first time, but I am as content right now as I think I might ever be.

And that's a good thing.

CHAPTER FOURTEEN
MONDAY, DECEMBER 21

I AWAKEN AND KNOW EXACTLY WHERE I AM.

It's court day.

And if it goes well, I'll be getting my company back.

Happy with that information, I get up and prepare for the day.

WE'RE WALKING from a parking garage to the Sam M. Gibbons United States Courthouse when it hits me.

"I've been here before."

Claire and Grady give me sideways glances that tell me they're dubious of my claim.

"I got called for federal jury duty. It was right after..." I pause, not wanting to finish my sentence. The truth is it was right after Claire and I had to end our relationship. "Nah," I finally continue. "I don't think I've been here after all."

"Do we know what's going to happen?" Grady asks. "Have you heard anything from Agent Hockenberry?"

"Nothing. I'm assuming they have a judge lined up who

will determine if I'm healthy enough to take over the company."

"And after that?"

"I kick Trevor out."

"And then?" Grady's asking questions that I've considered, but only in passing. Frankly, I doubted this moment would even get here, but it is here, and I've got decisions to make.

"Let's see what the judge says first."

We take an elevator to the fifth floor and check a directory to find the location of the courtroom where we're supposed to report. We're walking down the hall when I spot Trevor Stanley entering the room with four people I don't know. Stephanie and Randy are behind them.

And Michael is with them, too.

The sight of him with the other side makes my heart hurt. Grady and Claire see him, too. I hear Claire groan.

"What the hell?" Grady says. "Michael said he wanted to drive up by himself early this morning in your car. I didn't think it would be to meet with them."

"Maybe it's not what it appears to be," Claire says, taking my arm.

As she's speaking Michael turns and sees us. He glances back at his parents, then at us. He nods a solemn greeting, then follows them inside. I slow down so we won't all be trying to find seats at the same time. When we finally make it inside, I look around for Agent Hockenberry, but she's not there.

Her boss, Director Gwendolyn Abbott-Newsome, however, is seated on the front row of the gallery.

I can tell by the movements of Trevor's entourage that they're surprised to see a bigwig like the Director. The four strangers who entered the courtroom with Trevor huddle together, casting occasional glances over each other's shoulders at the FBI Director seated forty feet away. Director Newsome is oblivious as she consults with a woman in a navy business suit. When they see me, the woman waves and motions for me to join them. Claire and Grady follow me.

"Mr. Flanagan, I'm Kiara Kennedy. I'm an attorney referred to you by the Bureau."

"I didn't know that I needed an attorney. I don't even have any money."

While Ms. Kennedy explains her role, Director Newsome stands and exits the courtroom through a side door marked Private. I introduce Claire and Grady, then look across the aisle where Trevor and his suits are still huddled. My daughter, son-in-law, and grandson are seated in the row just behind them.

"It looks like they've got us outnumbered and outflanked," I say.

Ms. Kennedy glances at the gaggle and seems to dismiss them with a shake of her head.

"Outnumbered maybe, but right is always right. Join me at the table up front, please."

As we're getting seated, the judge enters and assumes his position on the bench. I'm struck by his uncanny resemblance to Michael Jordan, except he is wearing a robe instead of a basketball uniform. Trevor's troop takes their seats as the Judge shuffles papers for a few moments, then calls out a long case number. Ms. Kennedy stands and identifies herself, as does one of the suits across the aisle. His name is Bart Ackerman, and he's with the Tampa firm of Ackerman, Ackerman, and two names that aren't Ackerman. He appears to be perturbed as he speaks, as if he doesn't want to be here. Trevor and the others at his table are writing furiously on yellow legal pads. I wish I had thought to bring a yellow legal pad. Ms. Kennedy sees me admiring them, pulls one from her briefcase and hands it to me. I feel like a little boy in church whose mom brings a coloring book and crayons, except I don't have any crayons. Or a pen to write with. A moment later, she hands me that, too, a bright pink pen emblazoned with the name of a hair salon in Capitol Heights, Maryland, a place called *Fab's Hair Studio* that, according to the pen, specializes in *Custom Weaves, Relaxers, and Cuts*. Ms. Kennedy sees me reading the pen and tosses me a smile. I like her and hope she can win today.

The Judge states the reason for the hearing, which is to determine if the declaration originally signed by me to give Rosalie power of attorney over my business and personal decisions, then subsequently transferred to Stephanie after Rosalie's death can be overturned. Ms. Kennedy takes a few moments to explain to the Judge why I should be returned to the position of decision maker for my own affairs. She states, quite succinctly, that I was diagnosed with Alzheimer's, but have been mostly symptom-free for past couple weeks. She explains that I do have some issues with decreased cognitive awareness in the evenings, but my days have been clear and lucid.

Once she's seated, Trevor's man, Ackerman, begins to speak. He doesn't even bother to stand up, which I find rude and disrespectful. He provides a summary of my condition, reading from many of the same notes that were in my bedside table at Pinehurst Pavilion. He stresses that even my attorney, Ms. Kennedy, has acknowledged that I still have issues with diminished awareness as the day wears on.

"Not all decisions for a company as large as Flanagan Furniture are made in the light of day," he says. "What if a multi-million-dollar decision has to be made at eleven in the evening. How will Mr. Flanagan handle such situations?"

I have to admit that Ackerman has a point. I also have to admit that it's a point I have considered over the past couple days. I'm ready when called upon. I jot a note to Ms. Kennedy saying as much. She writes a response:

The Judge will determine if testimony is allowed.

Ackerman provides other information that he says speaks to my incapability to run a large company. He seems to have the Judge's ear, and I'm getting worried that a decision might be made without me getting to speak. Then, as arrogant men are wont to do sometimes, Ackerman steps in a pile of dog shit.

"It's a non-case, Your Honor. We have an elderly man with dementia. He's having moments of clarity, and he and his friends, one a former employee of the company, decide they want to make a money grab. They used Mr. Flanagan's name and reputation to rope in the FBI, who try to help them steal away the company from Mr. Flanagan's daughter and hand-chosen successor, Trevor Stanley. The fact that they hoodwinked this court to try a last-minute end run at a time when Mr. Stanley was out of the country is an abuse of the system."

Ackerman might've been okay had he not used the word, '*hoodwinked.*' I see a storm cloud flash across the Judge's face as the word is uttered. Even a couple of the suits on Trevor's side cast worried glances at their fearless leader. Oblivious, he picks a piece of lint off the cuff of his imported suit and smiles at his cronies. He's barely cognizant of the eruption brewing on the bench right in front of him.

"I can assure you, Mr. Ackerman, that this court has in no way, shape, or form been *hoodwinked.*"

The Judge's tone is at the same time level and bone-chilling. I'm reminded of my elementary school principal whose reprimands scared some of us kids so much that we would wet our pants. Ackerman's smug face crumbles as he scrambles to make sense of what's happening. He checks with the man seated next to him. I can read his lips as he whispers, "Did I say hoodwinked?" The man nods. Ackerman gets to his feet for the first time.

"Your Honor, by hoodwinked I meant the FBI was using its authority to—"

"The Federal Bureau of Investigation has no authority over this court, Mr. Ackerman. Did you not take junior high Civics?"

"What I meant to say was that my client was out of the country on vacation and faced a significant hardship, both emotionally and financially, to make it back in time for this trial."

The Judge nods. "Now I understand. Thank you for clarifying, Mr. Ackerman. Sit down."

Ackerman sits down. Whether I win or not, I have to admit that this is good theater. I wish Claire was sitting next to me, so I could write notes to her and her to me. I glance back and see her, and Grady, looking at me. Claire winks. That simple gesture makes me feel that everything is going to be okay.

"I would like to hear more arguments from both sides," the Judge says after a few moments. "Ms. Kennedy, would you like to go first?"

"I believe our case speaks for itself, Your Honor. We've submitted statements from FBI Field Agents Hockenberry, Cruz, and Hatcher attesting to Mr. Flanagan's mental state. I will pass on calling witnesses for the moment but would like to reserve the right to call them later if needed."

"Mr. Ackerman, do you have any further arguments against the petition?"

"We certainly do, Your Honor. I would like to begin by calling Mr. Flanagan's daughter, Stephanie Flanagan-Mott to the stand."

I shake my head sadly. It should never be like this, but Stephanie has forced the issue. She looks good, in a print skirt and white blouse, as she takes the stand. The man seated next to Ackerman, the one who confirmed for him that he had indeed said the court had been hoodwinked, stands.

"Ripley Snodgrass representing Flanagan Furniture," he says kindly. "I'll be deposing Mrs. Mott, if it pleases the court, Your Honor."

"Please proceed, Mr. Snodgrass."

I pick up my pink pen and jot, *Ripley Snodgrass is his real name?*

Ms. Kennedy offers the slightest of nods. Her attention is locked in on Stephanie. Behind me I hear a door open. Director Newsome has returned to the courtroom. She sits on the end of the row behind us, a few feet away from Claire.

Snodgrass takes a few minutes to elicit basic background information from Stephanie. She says nothing I haven't heard before. She tells how the company started, my involvement, our success, my decision to bring Trevor in. Then she talks about my illness, about how Rosalie took care of me at home, about how much of a hardship it presented. Rosalie comes across as a martyr, and for the most part, Stephanie is right. I hurt her mother, yet she took care of me until the day she died. No mention is made of my relationship with Claire.

Snodgrass asks a few more questions that allow

Stephanie to describe my illness. It started with little things, forgetting names, where I left things, how to get to certain familiar places in town, and progressed.

"My husband and I would've welcomed my father into our home, but he needed more care than we could provide. We spent months looking at care options before settling on Pinehurst Pavilion in Bradenton. It was in the community he knew and was staffed by caring people who had his best interests at heart."

That's her first lie. Grady has already told me otherwise.

Then, the second lie.

"We visited my father every chance we had, and always found him to be content and well-cared for."

I know from what I've heard and read that Stephanie rarely came to Pinehurst. I reach for my yellow legal pad to write this down for Ms. Kennedy, but she motions for me to hold on.

Snodgrass continues to draw Stephanie's story out. She speaks glowingly of Trevor and his leadership, about how the company has grown beyond anything it was before, and about how generous Trevor is with his time and money.

"Mrs. Mott, do you feel your father is capable of resuming control of Flanagan Furniture?"

Stephanie pulls at the hem of her skirt as she looks across the courtroom at me. A tear appears, then another. This surprises me. Stephanie has always been dramatic and prone to overreact. What she's not is a crier. I sense this is an act. Will the Judge?

"I love my father, but I'm not even sure he'll be mentally fit a half-hour from now, let alone in two days or two weeks. I shudder to think what will happen to Flanagan Furniture if he's given control."

It's Ms. Kennedy's turn to ask the questions, but the Judge says we're taking a break. He's barely out the door before Ms. Kennedy whispers, "You and your friends can go right through there." She points to the same side door that Director Newsome used earlier. "I'll come get you when we resume."

"How do you think we're doing?"

She gives me a thumbs-up, then stands and follows the Director out a rear door.

"Ms. Kennedy, please proceed."

The break was fifteen minutes. Claire, Grady, and I sat around a table covered with sticky coffee cup rings and decided that we had no idea if we were winning or losing. At one point I started to question if I really wanted to be in charge after all, but one look at Grady told me we were doing the right thing. The look of defeat I'd witnessed the day I surprised him at the factory is gone. He appears energized, and his energy becomes my energy.

Ms. Kennedy stands, thanks the Judge, and approaches Stephanie, stopping a few feet away to give her space.

"How often have you visited your father at Pinehurst Pavillion over the past six months, Mrs. Mott?"

"Not as often as I would like, given the distance between there and my home in Baltimore."

"Can you give us a number? Five times? Three? One?"

"Did you say in the last six months?"

"Yes, ma'am."

"We came down last week."

"That was after he left Pinehurst, correct, Mrs. Mott?"

"You mean after he escaped."

"How many times, Mrs. Mott?"

"None. Not in the last six months?"

"How about the past twelve months?"

Stephanie shakes her head, and I can see she's becoming exasperated.

"It's hard to say. We've been in constant touch with—"

"Just a number, Mrs. Mott."

"I'm not certain of the exact number, but I bet you know," Stephanie fires back.

"As a matter of fact, Mrs. Mott, I do. Do you want me to tell you?"

Stephanie doesn't answer. Ms. Kennedy waits a few beats, then looks to the Judge.

"Answer Ms. Kennedy's question, please."

"I wasn't able to see my father in person the past year."

Ms. Kennedy allows Stephanie's response to hang in the air for a bit while she returns to our table and pretends to look through some notes that I can see are not even related to my case. Satisfied that she's made her point, she moves back into the space between our table and Stephanie.

"You control a seventy percent stake in Flanagan Furniture, correct, Mrs. Mott?"

Stephanie glances at the suits seated around Trevor. Their faces are blank. She's on her own.

"The company is still in my father's name. It will pass to me upon his death. With the power of attorney he and Mom signed, I am responsible for seventy percent, yes."

"Do you look forward to the day when those shares are yours free and clear?"

"That's a stupid question," Stephanie says angrily. "Why would I want my father to die?"

"If your father means so much to you, Mrs. Mott, why haven't you visited him in over a year?" Ms. Kennedy withdraws the question just as Ackerman and Snodgrass shoot up from their seats to object, but I sense the damage has been done. There's no jury to play to, but Ms. Kennedy is intent on getting Stephanie off her stride. I admire her abilities as an attorney but wish Stephanie would see things from our perspective.

"Mrs. Mott, why did you assign your voting privileges to Mr. Stanley?"

Stephanie takes several slow breaths, then says, "I live a thousand miles away, so it's hard for me to be involved in the company's day-to-day operations. My father chose Trevor Stanley to ultimately replace him as President of Flanagan Furniture. If Trevor was good enough for him, he's good enough for me."

"What makes you think your father intended for Mr. Stanley to run the company?"

The question trips Stephanie up for a moment. She looks again at the people on her side, then glances at me. I shake my head. There's a flash of fear, but she seems to push it aside. "My father brought Trevor in and sold him part of the company. That indicates his intentions."

"What about Grady Longacre? He was also a shareholder, wasn't he?"

"Grady has struggled over the years. He had to sell his shares to Trevor when he got in financial trouble. He probably should've been fired, but Trevor kept him on, at least until recently. Grady lied to Trevor and had to be let go. Frankly, he should've done it sooner."

I expect Ms. Kennedy to probe more into Grady's role in the company, but she abruptly changes course.

"You receive compensation from Flanagan Furniture, don't you, Mrs. Mott?"

"I do."

"How much?"

When I hear the number Stephanie tosses out it makes my head spin. It's more than I paid myself as President.

"Mrs. Mott, what do you do to earn that much compensation?"

"It's my share of the company profits." Stephanie turns to speak to the Judge. "Profits are much higher than they used to be, thanks to Trevor."

"You say your payout is a share of the profits, but the amount you receive has remained the same. How can that be?"

Stephanie is stumped again. She's still considering her response when Ms. Kennedy moves on.

"Do you even know how profits have varied over the past few years?"

Ackerman jumps up again. "Your Honor, she's badgering Mrs. Mott."

"One question at a time, please, Ms. Kennedy."

Ms. Kennedy apologizes, then asks, "Do you review the company's financials?"

"Trevor has them sent to me."

"And you review them?"

"I keep them. I file them away with other company correspondence."

"So, you're saying you do not review them." Ms. Kennedy moves on before another objection can be raised.

"That's all I have, Your Honor."

"Any further witnesses, Mr. Ackerman?"

"I will be calling Trevor Stanley, Your Honor, but respectfully request a lunch break so we don't have to start and stop."

The Judge checks his watch. "It's eleven-twenty. We're adjourned until one."

Ms. KENNEDY DISAPPEARS with Director Newsome again, after telling us to go find some lunch and be back by one. I stop by the first row to get Grady and Claire.

"There's a nice deli two streets over," Claire says. The deli sounds great, and five minutes later we're enjoying the winter sunshine while walking up the street when a pair of Hillsborough County patrol cars pull up beside us. The drivers get out and approach.

"Are you Grady Longacre?" one asks Grady.

Grady says he is.

"You're under arrest for kidnapping," the deputy says as he shoves Grady against a street post. Grady doesn't resist.

"And you must be Mr. Flanagan?" the other deputy says. I acknowledge that I am, he tells me I'm under arrest, too. Now we're both handcuffed. The deputy who cuffed Grady opens the back door of his car, and we are both placed inside. For some reason we remain calm. Even Claire is taking this in with measured reserve.

"Where are you taking them?" she asks.

"To the Manatee County line," a deputy answers. "Their people will take over from there."

"I'll let Ms. Kennedy know," Claire says. "Take care of yourselves, guys. I don't imagine you'll be there long."

IT's obvious that the deputy who's escorting us back to Manatee County is not part of some bigger conspiracy. He warns us not to talk, then begins peppering us with questions. Grady respectfully tells him that it's probably better that we don't answer. He's good with that and quickly changes the conversation to college basketball, a topic Grady can speak of fluently, but I'm at a loss. We cross the Skyway Bridge and pull into a rest area where a Manatee County Sheriff's SUV is waiting. The cops exchange pleasantries while we are moved from one vehicle to the other. The deputy isn't a chatty sort, nor does he warn Grady and me to stay quiet, so we talk between ourselves.

"What do you think is happening back in Tampa?" I ask.

"Assuming Claire found your attorney and Director Newsome, I suspect all hell is breaking loose," Grady says.

"Maybe Agent Hockenberry or one of the others will be waiting to spring us," I offer hopefully. "I hate to miss my own hearing."

Traffic is heavy, and it's after one when we reach the Manatee County Sheriff's headquarters behind an old shopping mall in midtown Bradenton. Grady and I are processed, and our handcuffs are removed, then we're sent off in different directions. I'm placed in a room about the size of a walk-in closet, given a bottle of water, and told that a detective will be in shortly to visit with me.

Two hours later I'm still waiting. I get up and try to open the door, but it's locked. I need a restroom. I bang on the door, but no one answers. I sit back down and wait. Thirty minutes later a man enters who is the prototype of every TV police detective. Balding, chubby, with an ill-fitting sport coat, he says his name is Dameron. I ask for the restroom and he has someone come and take me. Ten minutes later we're back together. I'm no cop or lawyer, but I've watched plenty of shows about them, so I know not to offer anything.

"We're looking for a woman named Sita," Dameron says. "Where can we find her?"

"I want my lawyer."

"Is she still alive?"

"I want my lawyer."

"Look, Mr. Flanagan." Dameron relaxes in his chair as if we're old friends. "We have reason to suspect that Grady Longacre is the actual kidnapper. You were only along for the ride. If that's the case, let me know and we can make a deal."

"My lawyer's name is Kiara Kennedy. Call her at the federal courthouse in Tampa."

Dameron's back on his feet. He shoves his chair under the table with enough force to make the walls shake. Intimidation tactics, just like the TV shows. I smile and repeat, "Kiara Kennedy." Dameron glares at me, then exits the room.

It's five-fifty in the afternoon and I'm getting worried. I haven't eaten since breakfast and the headache I've come to associate with my nocturnal regression is pressing in. I bang on the door again, but no one answers. I shout, but no one replies.

CHAPTER FIFTEEN
TUESDAY, DECEMBER 22

I AWAKEN AND KNOW EXACTLY WHERE I AM.

Claire's place. In her bed. She's standing in the doorway looking at me. There's concern on her face. And happiness. I choose to acknowledge the happiness.

"Good morning, sweetheart."

She flashes her best smile, but it disappears quickly.

"How's your head?"

"Now that you mention it, it kinda hurts." I reach up and feel a huge goose egg "What happened?"

"They put you in county lockup. Another prisoner jumped you. He only had a few seconds before the guards pulled him off, but you hit your head on the toilet. You were taken to Manatee Memorial and checked out. By the time they were ready to release you, Agents Cruz and Hatcher had arrived. They got you released to me."

Tears well up in Claire's eyes. I reach for her hand, but she bypasses that and lies down next to me and nestles close. "I was scared the trauma might set you back. I've not slept a wink. I've prayed and prayed that you would come back to me."

"And here I am," I say brightly, hugging her with every-thing I have. "I've been given another day."

"Yeah," Claire says. "But we have to spend it back in court. We leave in an hour."

"We're not taking any chances today," Agent Christine Hockenberry says as she holds open the door to a work-issued gray sedan. Claire and I are sitting in back. Grady is already seated up front.

Claire has spent the last hour filling me in on what took place after I faded away last night. The assault, the trip to ER. It's no surprise that it was Trevor who filed the report that led to our arrest.

"We anticipate that he'll be testifying today that the two of you were responsible for Sita's disappearance," Hocken-berry tells us on the drive to Tampa. "And if he does, boy do we have a surprise for him."

"One thing I still don't understand," I say. "Why is Director Newsome in town? She doesn't appear to be directly involved with the case. She stepped out several times yesterday morning. Wouldn't her time be better spent on something more important?"

"Anything I can offer would only be speculation, Mr. Flanagan. The Director has barely spoken to me, and she's known throughout the Bureau as a boss who keeps her distance from her employees." Hockenberry pauses to check traffic as she merges onto a Tampa freeway. "But it would appear that your friendship with her husband has some meaning to her."

I'm touched and don't know what to say. Claire

squeezes my hand and gives me a smile that tells me she's proud of me.

"He always was a schmoozer," Grady says, looking over the seat at me. "It must be those fancy seersucker suits. I'm going to have to get me a couple of those when this is all over."

KIARA KENNEDY IS ALREADY SEATED when we enter the courtroom. She winces when she sees the bandage on the back of my head, then motions to the seat next to her. Trevor and his gang haven't yet made their appearance.

"I tripped," I joke.

"Or something like that," Ms. Kennedy says as she pats my hand. "Your arrest at lunch caused quite the stir. The Judge reluctantly postponed the afternoon session, but we're going to have to make sure he knows who the real culprit is."

"How do you plan to do that?"

"Trevor Stanley is a very complicated person. He's a proud, vain man." Ms. Kennedy lowers her voice. "I don't believe that he's told his attorneys the real story about the domestic worker you rescued from his home. If they're aware of the circumstances, there's no way they'll put him on the stand this morning."

"And if he does testify?" I ask.

"Then it will be a bloodbath, Mr. Flanagan. And the blood will be Trevor Stanley's."

As we're speaking Trevor enters the courtroom with his attorneys and the other suits. He looks at me as if I'm a cockroach, pauses like he wants to say something, but is guided away by Ackerman. After he gets everyone seated,

Ackerman crosses the aisle and says to Ms. Kennedy, "Anything we need to discuss before getting started?"

"Not here. You're the one who should be answering that question, Mr. Ackerman. Having my client arrested during lunch was quite a stunt."

"Yeah, well you never know when law enforcement will strike, do you? You need to know, Miss Kennedy, that if Mr. Flanagan here intends to testify, we will pound away on his involvement with the kidnapping of Mr. Stanley's maid. The Judge deserves to know the truth."

"Mr. Ackerman, do you really think the maid's disappearance was a kidnapping? That she was taken against her will?"

Ackerman shrugs. "It wouldn't surprise me if she was in on it from the start. Trevor says she was becoming difficult to deal with. It's not much different than my experiences with any of them, to be honest."

Ms. Kennedy stiffens. "Who do you mean when you say *any of them?*"

"Domestics, gardeners. Especially those from out of the country. They come here looking for instant wealth and prosperity, then, when they don't find it, they convince someone to help them start over. I've seen it before."

Ms. Kennedy nods to the rear of the courtroom. Director Newsome has just walked in. She makes brief eye contact with the attorneys, offers me a grim smile, and moves down the aisle to the spot she occupied yesterday.

"Have you wondered why she's here?" Ms. Kennedy asks Ackerman.

"We're not stupid, Ms. Kennedy. We know about her family relationship with your client." Ackerman pauses, shakes his head, then leans in closer. "What's surprising is how she's willing to throw so much agency time and manpower into something as insignificant as this."

I can't believe what I'm hearing. He has no idea, but that doesn't stop him from continuing to talk.

"You guys have probably been trying to find some illegalities with the way Trevor conducts company business overseas, but I can assure you that he's clean. If there was even a whiff of impropriety our firm wouldn't touch him with a ten-foot pole. We don't need the business."

Ms. Kennedy nods. I'm all ears for what she says next. She doesn't disappoint.

"It's not his *company* dealings we're concerned about. It's much more involved than that."

She's knocked Ackerman off his game. He gives her a quizzical look, starts to say something, but is interrupted by the Judge's arrival.

"It's time to depose Mr. Stanley," Ms. Kennedy says as a parting shot. "You never know what we might learn."

As the Judge sorts through his notes and prepares to call us to order, I watch the whispered discussions at the table to our right. Ackerman is doing most of the talking, all of it directed at Trevor. Several times I see him look over the attorney's shoulder in our direction. He appears concerned. Then, when I see him look back at Director Newsome, I know he's concerned. He has the look of a man who's been caught in a lie.

"We'll get started now," the Judge says. "Mr. Ackerman, you were planning to call Mr. Stanley to the stand after yesterday's lunch recess. Please proceed."

I sense that everything we've come here for is hanging in the balance. Will Ackerman allow his client to be questioned, or will his concerns for what he doesn't know cause him to pull the plug? And if he does decide to take a pass on

Trevor testifying, what evidence can he offer that will swing things their way?

"Mr. Ackerman? The Court is waiting."

Ackerman gets to his feet. Slowly. Buying time.

"Your Honor, if it pleases the Court, I would like to rearrange our order of testimony. We have two experts in the field of Alzheimer's and dementia who I think can convince the court why Mr. Flanagan is unfit to reassume his role in the company."

The Judge appears perplexed for a moment, but it passes. "Please proceed."

The next ninety minutes drag by as the men who have been in court with Trevor the past two days take turns on the stand. Their credentials are impeccable, and their testimonies mirror each other's. Recovery from dementia and Alzheimer's, particularly in the advanced stages I demonstrated prior to my escape from Pinehurst Pavilion, is always temporary, and patients can regress without notice. They cite studies from home and abroad that confirm their statements.

For all intents and purposes, I shouldn't be sitting here.

But dammit, I am.

And that's the direction Ms. Kennedy takes when it's her turn to question the experts.

"If everything you've told us is true," she politely asks the first expert, "how do you explain Mr. Flanagan's current condition?"

"It's an anomaly," he says. "It won't last."

"How do you know that?"

"It never does."

"You've seen cases like Mr. Flanagan's, where people formerly suffering from dementia have had extended periods of clarity?"

"Define 'extended periods.'"

"We have witnesses who will testify that this is his eleventh day of clarity."

"Then, no, I haven't seen a case like that."

"If you've not encountered a case like Mr. Flanagan's, then how do you know he'll regress?"

The doctor removes his glasses, wipes them with a handkerchief, and says, "Because they always do."

Ms. Kennedy speaks more to the Judge than the expert when she says, "it seems we're going in circles. I'm done."

She repeats the same line of questioning with the second witness, and while he dodges being pinned down like the first, he still has to admit that mine is an extraordinary situation.

"We're going to break for lunch," the Judge says when the second expert exits the witness stand. "Will Mr. Stanley be ready to testify when we return, Mr. Ackerman?"

I've watched the notes flying back and forth during the experts' depositions. I expect that Trevor has had to disclose some unpleasant facts with his legal team. Now, the question remains, what will their next step be?

Trevor is gone.

Attorney Ackerman is gone.

So are Stephanie and Randy.

And Michael.

FBI Director Newsome is gone, too.

Ripley Snodgrass, the genial second stringer who deposed Stephanie has moved into the main chair. The two experts on dementia have flown the coop, so it's just Snodgrass. All alone.

I'm starting to worry that Ms. Kennedy has disappeared as well, but one minute before court is scheduled to resume, she hustles in and sits down beside me.

"Sudden change in plans," she whispers. "Bear with me and we'll be done in an hour."

I want to ask questions, but she's busy writing away on her legal pad, so I let it slide.

The Judge returns, takes a look at the empty seats, then proceeds as if nothing is different. Snodgrass stands, waits to be acknowledged, then says, "I'll be handing this matter for the duration, Your Honor."

"Proceed, Mr. Snodgrass."

"We have no further testimony, Your Honor."

"Very well. Ms. Kennedy?"

"I would like to call Grady Longacre to the stand."

Grady had no idea this was coming. I know that because we enjoyed lunch together at a Chik-Fil-A three blocks away. Just to be sure I didn't fade out and dream it, I check the lapel of his sport coat. Yep, the buffalo dipping sauce stain is right there.

"Mr. Longacre, tell the court about your life over the past few years." That's all Kiara Kennedy has to say. Grady talks about the good times at Flanagan Furniture, back when we worked together. He discusses my gradual slide and the moment when everyone knew they had to remove me from my position with the company. He describes Trevor's ascent to the top of the organizational chart and about the excesses and trappings he created for himself along the way. He grows teary talking about the day he had to sell his share in the company to Trevor and about how Trevor minimized him day by day.

"I used to be acknowledged and appreciated," Grady says, not bothering to wipe away the tears that fall to his cheeks. "After Trevor took over, I was denigrated and humiliated."

"Would it be fair to say that you do not like Trevor Stanley?" Ms. Kennedy asks.

"I despise him."

"Now, Mr. Longacre, tell us about Mr. Stanley's housekeeper, Sita."

As Grady unpacks the story of Sita and her son I see the first sign of emotion on the Judge's face. He's done a good job of playing his cards close to the vest, but the horrid account of a child's drowning is hard to hear. It's a sad story of unnecessary death, and when Grady finishes telling it the courtroom is quiet.

"Your Honor," Ms. Kennedy says as she returns to our table. "I have a sworn statement from the housekeeper. Mr. Longacre and Mr. Flanagan knew what she was facing and rescued her from Trevor Stanley's house last week. She's in a safe house now, where she's being given time to decide what her next step will be." She hands the statement to the Judge and Attorney Snodgrass. They take a few moments to read it, and I can see from both men's expressions that the account is difficult to parse.

"Your Honor, you see the name, Victor Ballentine on Page Three of the statement. Mr. Ballentine was an employee of Trevor Stanley's. He was arrested early this morning at his home for sexual assault. Sita's account of his repeated attacks are included in the statement."

More silence as the men continue to read. Snodgrass's shoulders slump as he flips from page to page. I suspect he is the conscious of Ackerman, Ackerman, and the rest. Why he chooses to associate with an ass like Ackerman is beyond me, but it's his bed so he's going to have to lie in it.

The Judge prompts Ms. Kennedy to proceed.

"Mr. Longacre tell us about the past eleven days. Specifically, your time with Mr. Flanagan."

This part of the testimony is happier, more upbeat. Grady describes our time together, everything from our first lunch at the Star Fish Company to the conversations and reminiscing the three of us enjoyed in my living room. He also talks about how I fade late in the day. Grady's holding nothing back, and I'm gratified he isn't.

"Do you feel Mr. Flanagan is clear of mind as we sit here today?" Ms. Kennedy asks as a final question.

"Undoubtedly. He's as much the old Neal as he was fifteen years ago. I'm glad to have my friend back."

When called to cross-examine, Snodgrass stands and says, "Thank you, Mr. Longacre. No questions."

He steps away and Ms. Kennedy calls Dr. Patterson. The doctor appears through a side door, accompanied by an attorney of his own. I'm surprised and dubious. Ms. Kennedy charges ahead. She walks Patterson through his background, then gets to the point of his appearance.

"I'm here because I agreed to cooperate with state and federal authorities."

"Are you avoiding prison time for your cooperation?"

"Probably not. I've been told that I could serve between three and seven years, but that's a lot less than what I would face otherwise." Patterson's stoicism fades as he says, "At least I'll get to see my kids again, I hope."

Patterson proceeds to drop the bomb that blows the other side's case out of the water. Trevor Stanley came to him with a proposal to keep me institutionalized until it could be confirmed that I had slipped permanently back into the throes of dementia.

"He presented Mr. Flanagan as an individual who was a danger to himself and others."

"After examining him did you conclude this was the case?"

"No, ma'am. I found a man who was in complete control of his senses during the day. He suffers from what we call sundowning but emerges from it each morning."

"Yet you planned to administer medications that would keep him in a state of impairment?"

"I did, and that's why I'm going to jail."

The rest of Patterson's testimony is clinical, using lingo and terms to describe what he's already said. Like Ackerman's experts, he admits he's never experienced a case like mine, but readily admits that there are often things in the field of medicine that cannot be explained.

"Sometimes we have to accept that miracles happen," he says. I like that. Miracles are good, particularly if they happen to you.

And finally, Ms. Kennedy asks, "What role did Mr. Flanagan's daughter play in your decision to accept him in your facility?"

"None directly. When we visited, she said that she would go along with whatever Trevor Stanley felt was best."

That makes me feel good, too. At least Stephanie hasn't knowingly sent me off to die. Of course, the fact that she agreed to having me sent off at all is still working against her.

Patterson is dismissed without any cross-examination from Snodgrass. I think we're done, but Ms. Kennedy has one more ace up her sleeve.

"I call Neal Flanagan to the stand."

The Judge gives me a sympathetic look as I climb into the seat next to him. I smile in return. Ms. Kennedy comes forward and gets right to the point.

"Mr. Flanagan are you able to reassume control of your company?"

"Yes," I answer quickly. "But I don't want it."

Every eye in the place is on me. I've thrown a curveball that even my lawyer wasn't expecting. I owe it to her to elaborate, so I do.

"If the power of attorney I signed years ago is rescinded, I'll call a meeting of the company shareholders. We will—"

"By shareholders, you mean yourself?"

"I will control seventy percent of the company. Trevor Stanley maintains the other thirty percent."

"Mr. Stanley probably won't be attending that meeting," Snodgrass interjects, an uneasy grin crossing his face.

"At that meeting I will fire any and all of Trevor Stanley's employees who aren't actually doing work for the company. I'll end the company's relationship with the overseas companies where the cheap crap furniture they're selling now is made."

I pause, take a sip of water from a glass offered by Ms. Kennedy, then proceed. "I'll list the new part of the building with a local realtor. I'm not current on commercial real estate trends, but I anticipate we can get a couple million dollars for it. If it doesn't sell, we can lease it. Either way, that glass and brick testament to Trevor Stanley's short-sighted leadership will generate income that will give us time to get back to what we do best."

"Which is what, Mr. Flanagan?"

"Top quality furniture that comes with a lifetime warranty. The kind that our customers used to line up for."

As I'm speaking the rear door opens and Michael comes in. He scans the room, then takes a seat next to Claire. The two of them begin to whisper between themselves while Ms. Kennedy continues.

"We will dedicate our time and energy to regaining our former customers' trust. We will tool up our old factory and begin producing furniture. It will take some time, but I firmly believe that the business model we followed for so many years can still be successful today."

"But what if you don't have much time?"

Ms. Kennedy's question surprises me. I might've expected it from the other side of the aisle, but not from my own lawyer. Then I realize, it's the perfect question. Kiara Kennedy is a genius, and she's just teed it up for me to hit out of the park.

"I probably don't have a few years. I might not have more than a few days, but I've considered that." I look back at where Grady is seated next to Claire and Michael. I smile at Grady and say, "I'll immediately name my longtime friend, Grady Longacre, as President of Flanagan Furniture. It's a position he should've had years ago."

Grady tears up again. The man is such a wuss. I look from him to Claire and Michael. They've just concluded whatever they were discussing, and Claire looks at me and gives me a thumbs-up. That's all I need to say what's been on my heart since my grandson first walked into my room at Patterson's facility.

"I'll appoint my grandson, Michael Mott, as Sales Manager. He'll need to put every waking moment into winning back our customers, but I know he can do it. Eventually he'll take over. I may not be around, but the thought of my grandson leading the company is a dream I've had since he was a baby. This will ensure it happens."

Michael appears overjoyed at this announcement. Claire does, too.

"I'll update my will to ensure that Flanagan Furniture remains in the family when I'm gone. Michael will inherit most of my share. A portion will go to the two people who have stood by since I returned." I don't need to say Claire and Grady's names. Everyone knows who I'm talking about.

"It appears you've given this transition a lot of thought... a lot of rational thought."

Ms. Kennedy's statement is for the benefit of the Judge. And she's right. I have given it a lot of thought.

After Ms. Kennedy returns to her seat, the Judge asks Snodgrass if he has questions. He rises, adjusts his lapels, and approaches. I'm ready for whatever he plans to dish out.

"Mr. Flanagan, a lot has come to light over the past twenty-four hours." He looks up to the Judge and continues. "There is a lot about our client that we didn't know, and we're still discovering more every minute."

He's being quite magnanimous, but I still don't trust him.

"No one can say for sure how long you'll remain in your present frame of mind, Mr. Flanagan. Personally, I still believe that your return could be detrimental to Flanagan Furniture. That said, I admire the way you've considered the future, and since it appears that I no longer have a client to represent in this matter, our firm has no objection to having the power of attorney rescinded."

Snodgrass takes a seat, and the courtroom grows quiet for several moments. The Judge is reading through a pile of paper, looking for what, I have no idea. He finally looks up.

"Typically, a decision like this would be rendered only after several days of consideration. I feel that I owe that much to both parties."

He pauses for effect. My stomach is lurching.

"In this case, however, given what we've learned about Mr. Stanley's personal and professional life, I'm comfortable with immediate termination of the power of attorney that was granted to your daughter, Stephanie Flanagan-Mott and assigned to Trevor Stanley. Effective immediately, Mr. Flanagan, your company is, once again, your company."

He bangs his gavel and flashes the first real smile I've seen from the bench. "Happy Holidays, Mr. Flanagan. May your Christmas be a clear Christmas."

It's after four when we settle into a corner table at Tampa's famous Bern's Steak House. They've just opened for the evening, and the place is filling up fast. We didn't have reservations, but someone has pulled some strings, because no one walks into Bern's without a reservation. I suspect that Director Newsome is behind it, but don't ask.

Ms. Kennedy comes to the booth with Claire, Grady, Michael, and me, orders a vodka and tonic, and downs it like a sailor just off the ship. The waiter brings menus thicker than some books I've read. Ms. Kennedy declines. "I've got a plane to catch in two hours," she says. "I just wanted to get you folks settled before I go."

"Have you got time to answer some questions?" I ask.

"Shoot."

"What will happen to Trevor?"

"Let me get another drink first." She flags down the waiter, orders, then starts talking.

"As we suspected, he had been less than forthcoming with his attorneys. When they figured out that we had him in our crosshairs for the housekeeper he tried to make a run for it at lunch."

"Seriously?"

"Yep. Why he thought he could outrun the FBI is

beyond me, but he tried. Agent Cruz nabbed him coming off the Selmon Expressway."

This is crazy. I can see that Grady and Claire are as shocked as I am. Michael, not so much.

"You knew?" I ask him.

"Mom and Dad asked me to sit with them in court. They promised me that information would come out that proved that they were right to keep you locked away." He pauses and looks down at his lap. "Grandpa, I'm sorry, but I felt I owed them that much."

I tell him that I understand.

"Mom wasn't involved with the stuff Mr. Stanley had going on. If she's guilty of anything it's letting greed cloud her judgment."

"Michael's right," Ms. Kennedy says. "The Bureau has nothing on your daughter and her husband."

"Still," Michael says slowly. "She didn't support you over the past few years. You shouldn't feel bad about leaving her and Dad out of your plans."

That's an awfully mature thing for him to say. It would be easy enough to hold a grudge, but Stephanie will always be my daughter. Nothing should change that, and nothing will change that.

"I'm giving her a small share of the company," I say. The others seem surprised, except Claire. I see her nodding in agreement. "Those shares will be controlled by the two of you." I motion to Grady and Michael. "I want her to be comfortable as she ages, and I suspect with you in charge she will be."

Ms. Kennedy asks if we have more questions. We don't, so she knocks back the last of her drink, gets to her feet, and says, "Dinner is already paid for. Don't worry about who picked up the check, just enjoy." I get up to shake her hand. She hugs me instead. And then she's gone.

The food arrives and it's perfect. Grady orders wine and drinks too much. Claire has a couple glasses, too. Michael and I abstain. Michael will be driving us back to Bradenton. And me? I'm feeling a headache coming on.

CHAPTER SIXTEEN
WEDNESDAY, DECEMBER 23

I AWAKEN AND KNOW EXACTLY WHERE I AM.

And what I need to do.

Before tomorrow.

But the question is, how? How am I going to do what I need to do before tomorrow? I'll need help to pull it off, but I would prefer to leave those closest to me out of this. It's not that I can't depend on Claire, Grady, or Michael, it's just that I need to do this myself.

I'm mulling over what has to be done when Claire enters the bedroom with a cup of coffee. It's barely past seven, but she's already dressed and ready for the day. I know she's planning on spending it with me, but I'm going to have to disappoint her this one time.

"Good morning, sleepy head!" she greets me in sing-song voice. "Want to go out for breakfast?"

"Sit down, sweetheart," I say, patting the bed next to me.

GRADY IS WAITING for me at the front door of the factory. I'm certain he's already heard from Claire. It was touch and go for a few minutes, as I worked to convince her that I had something to do that could only be done alone. I still don't know how I'm going to pull it off, but somehow, I must.

"Don't say a word," I say as he holds the front door open. "Do you have it?"

Grady holds up a company credit card embossed with the Flanagan Furniture name. Technically, since the Judge ruled in my favor yesterday, I'm free to use the card.

"Make sure to alert the credit card company that all other cards are to be shut off," I say as I take the card from his hand. "The only working card will be this one, at least for now."

"Already done. Now, do you want to tell me what you're doing?"

"I can't, Grady."

"I don't like you driving around without a license, especially in that old car of yours. We don't even know if it's roadworthy."

I glance back at the Riviera and remember how much I loved driving it when Rosalie and I purchased it twenty-some years ago. "She'll do fine," I say. "I'm not going far."

That's a lie. I'm going very far, just not in the Riviera.

I PULL out of the factory lot and am officially flying by the seat of my pants. Is it even possible to do what I need to do? I'm about to find out, but first I need gasoline. I pull into the Wawa in front of Rock and Redeemer Church, pull out the credit card, insert it into the pump, and start filling the tank. While I'm there I see a car pull into the church parking lot several hundred yards away. The driver's door opens, and Pastor Lonnie scrambles out. It's the first time I've seen a small person driving a car. Does he have special controls? Are the foot pedals raised up to seat level? These are questions that shouldn't be filling my mind at the moment, but I can't help myself.

And then, as I'm replacing the gas tank cover and getting back in the Riviera, I have an idea. If it works, it will help my plan come together. I drive to the church lot and pull up behind Pastor Lonnie's car. He is getting something out of his trunk, which takes some real dexterity. When he turns around and sees me, he smiles, and I can tell he remembers me.

"Your name is Gary, right?" he says.

Maybe he doesn't remember me after all.

"No, Pastor, my name is—"

"Just kidding you, Neal. How are you doing?"

"Pretty good, Pastor Lonnie. How are you?"

"C'mon buddy, you practically burned rubber getting over here from Wawa. How are you *really* doing?"

So much for small talk. Do all preachers cut right to the chase like this?

"Well, since you're asking, I was wondering if you might have some time to help me with something?"

He doesn't look at his watch or scan the horizon. He doesn't take a few minutes to come up with excuses. He just says, "I can free myself up all day. What do you need?"

"Want to go on a little trip?"

I'VE BEEN with Pastor Lonnie for twenty minutes before I slip and cuss.

We're at the ticket counter at Sarasota-Bradenton airport, when the representative tells me it will take me eleven hours to get to Baltimore.

"I don't have eleven hours."

"Then you're not going to Baltimore."

That's when I cuss. As soon as it slips out, I look at Pastor Lonnie. He winks, then steps in and takes over.

"Ma'am, I'm a pastor. This man has to get to Baltimore today." Pastor Lonnie shakes his head sadly as he continues. "He has cancer... of the earlobes."

The representative, a young lady of maybe twenty-five, gasps. "I'm so sorry," she says, looking from my earlobes to Pastor Lonnie. She's probably on the verge of a full-blown panic attack. How often does she encounter a customer with earlobe cancer traveling with a dwarf who is also a Mighty Man of God? She looks to her left, then to her right, then her face brightens. She leans close and motions for me to do the same. She points down the row of ticket counters, to one that I've never heard of before.

"They leave for Baltimore in forty minutes," she whispers. "Non-stop. If my supervisor hears me telling you this, I'll be shit-canned for sure." Like me, she looks down at Pastor Lonnie after her slip of the tongue.

"I've never heard of that airline," I whisper back.

"I have," Pastor Lonnie says. "They just started flying in here. Let's go."

I cuss again at the security counter, when I'm asked for a valid form of identification.

"I don't have a driver's license."

The security gal, a stern looking sort with a badge that

says she's part of something called TSA, looks me over from head to toe.

"What form of identification do you have, then?"

The only thing I've got on me is the company credit card and thirty-seven dollars. And one of Agent Christine Hockenberry's business cards. The credit card doesn't satisfy the security lady, so I hand her Agent Hockenberry's card.

"Can you call her?"

Pastor Lonnie steps forward again. "It's very important."

This is the first time that the security lady realizes we're together. "Do you have ID?"

Pastor Lonnie smiles. "I got more ID cards than the fifth grade has spitballs. What do you want to see? Driver's license? YMCA pass? Here's my preacher's identification card. It gets me the best parking spots at all the local hospitals and nursing homes."

I'm starting to think this isn't going to work. We're twenty-four minutes from our plane taking off and on the wrong side of the security queue. The lady considers us for a couple minutes, says something into a walkie talkie on her shoulder, then motions for us to follow her. We're taken to a quiet area of the airport, Pastor Lonnie to one room, me to another. A different security person comes in, introduces himself, and proceeds to ask me every question under the sun. Age, birthdate, family members, occupation, everything. He asks if I've been out of the country in the past year. Of course, I haven't. Then he asks why I have Agent Hockenberry's card. I tell him I just got done helping the FBI with an important case. He appears doubtful, but I press on.

"Just call her. She can tell you."

But he doesn't call. Instead, he actually lets me go. When I get to the gate, Pastor Lonnie is waiting. Our plane is boarding.

WE'RE CRAMMED in like sardines, but fortunately Pastor Lonnie doesn't take up much space. We spend the duration of the two-hour flight getting acquainted. He's naturally curious as to why I needed him to come along, so I tell him. I spring for snacks when they bring the cart around, pretzels and Diet Coke for the pastor, cookies and Sprite for me. I explain to him why we're going to Baltimore. He's a special person, Pastor Lonnie, and I can already see that his being with me is going to make all the difference. Especially if our return flight gets back after I sundown.

WE USE Pastor's driver's license and my credit card to get a rental car. I drive. It's an economy car with the get-up of an old hound dog. The rental agent gives us a map that's impossible to read, but Pastor has a map on his phone that we use to find our way to Stephanie's place.

She's surprised when I call and tell her I'm in town. She says she just got back herself late last night. When I ask if I can come see her, she's reluctant at first. I try explaining, but she seems not to want to see me. That hurts. I'm about to give up when Pastor Lonnie takes the phone.

"Hey, Stephanie, my name is Lonnie. I'm a friend of your Dad's. You don't know me, but please listen anyway." He tells her in excruciating detail every obstacle we've had to overcome to get to Baltimore before noon. His voice is pleasant and, more importantly, convincing. Stephanie tells us to come over.

IT's one-fifteen when we ring Stephanie's doorbell. I've been here before. Not as often as Rosalie used to come, but several times. The neighborhood is nice. The house used to be mortgaged to the hilt, but I expect she and Randy have put some of their Flanagan money toward paying things off.

Stephanie answers the door, considers Pastor Lonnie and me, then steps aside to let us in.

"I'll wait outside," Pastor says. I go in alone.

"Dad, this is ridiculous. Why would you fly all this way in your condition?"

"I need to talk to you."

She points to the living room. "Randy's working. I have an appointment in a little while, so we need to make this quick."

Her tone is measured, guarded. Not like one talks to family, unless they're on the outs with that family. I take a seat on the sofa. Stephanie sits in an uncomfortable looking wingback chair across the room. I wish we were closer, in more ways than one.

I decide to try Pastor Lonnie's approach of getting right to the point.

"I'm sorry things are like this between us."

Stephanie throws up her hands. "You made them this way."

"I cheated on your mother. That was wrong."

"You're damn right it was wrong. You crushed her."

"What can I do to make it right with you?"

She laughs harshly. "It's a little late for that, isn't it?"

"I don't know. Is it? Can we never be close again?"

She shakes her head, then checks her watch. I try to come up with what to say next. Part of me wants to defend myself, let Stephanie know that her mother wasn't completely without blame for the problems in our marriage. I don't, though. That would be too easy. And wrong. Nope, regardless of how things changed between Rosalie and me, I'm the one who had the affair.

"Michael has become a fine young man," I say, searching for common ground.

"He's a lot like you," Stephanie says, softer now. "Or like you used to be."

"Tomorrow I'll be naming him Sales Manager of Flanagan Furniture. He'll run the place in a few years."

"I'll bet you're happy you got the company back."

"I'd be happier if I had my daughter back."

The room becomes quiet. I hope I've broken through, at least a little, but Stephanie has become a hardened version of her younger self. We sit there for several moments, neither saying anything, then she checks her watch again.

"I have to go, Dad."

PASTOR LONNIE DOESN'T PROD, and I don't provide much information. We arrive back at the airport at three-fifteen and barely make another discount nonstop flight to Sarasota. We're preparing to land when he asks if there's anything I want him to pray for. I tell him about our meeting tomorrow morning, and about my plans for the company. He promises to be in full-on prayer mode all morning. We land at ten past six, and I'm starting to feel a headache coming on. Pastor asks if I want him to drive me home. I say no, that I can make it.

And I do make it. I walk into the house at six-forty, exhausted, my trip a complete and utter failure. Claire meets me and asks how my day was. She doesn't pry. She's respectful of my need to keep at least one thing to myself. I promise myself that it will be the last secret I'll ever keep from her. She brings me a bowl of tomato soup with crackers, and I begin eating. The headache is building, though.

CHAPTER SEVENTEEN
CHRISTMAS EVE

I AWAKEN AND KNOW EXACTLY WHERE I AM.

The disappointment of my previous day's trip has been washed away by something else.

Excitement.

It's going to be a very special day, perhaps the most special of my life, only to be eclipsed by tomorrow. I hope.

Special because I plan to reorganize Flanagan Furniture into the company it once was.

Special because I plan to turn over the reins to my best friend.

Special because I am providing a future for my only grandson.

And special because I'm going to ask Claire to marry me.

Sure, I've asked her before, but this time is for real.

And if she says yes, we'll get married tomorrow.

Between now and the moment I ask her, which I plan to do just before noon, there is so much to be done. Grady has set the wheels in motion, making arrangements with the people who will be needed to pull off a one-day trans-formation.

We'll begin at nine. It's seven-fifteen. That gives me at least forty-five minutes to roll over and curl into my still dozing Claire.

WE CHOOSE the old conference room next to my former office to hold the meeting. Grady had one of the company custodians clear it out last night. It smells musty and unused, but that's fine. In the coming months I expect it will get plenty of use.

At five minutes before nine I walk in and take the seat at the head of the conference table. It's the same chair I used when I still worked, and I smile when I realize it still conforms to my backside. I instruct Grady to sit on my left and Michael on my right. Since Betsy, my former secretary, is long-retired and relocated to Rhode Island to be near her grandkids, Grady has arranged for a young woman named Ashton to keep minutes of our meeting. Ashton, he tells me, recently started work at Flanagan Furniture and is the only person close to Trevor's inner sanctum who can be trusted. If he's right, she'll remain as his Executive Assistant. Grady insists on calling her that, rather than secretary. It's the way things are now, he says. Personally, I think it's sad. The position of secretary used to be a plumb job filled by talented and trusted employees. I'll not raise a fuss, though. It's like my long-ago buddy Jimmy Ingram used to say: not my monkey, not my circus.

The seat next to Michael is occupied by our new legal counsel. During my years running the company, I trusted my legal matters to a distant cousin who ran a small firm here in Bradenton. Bobby Zucker passed away six years ago, I'm saddened to discover, but his son Lawrence is running the firm now. Lawrence is a smart and gregarious young guy who is delighted with the chance to regain our business.

The only person missing is Claire. I had assumed she was coming along, but she surprised me this morning by electing to stay at the house. "You have a lot of cleaning up to do," she said as she laid next to me. "You need Grady and Michael today, not me." I reminded her that I needed her every minute of every day, but she still chose to stay back.

At nine on the nose I glance toward the conference room door. I had a dream last night, one I actually remember, that Trevor Stanley showed up at the last minute in an attempt to railroad our plans. I shared the dream with Grady this morning. He made a quick call to Agent Christine Hockenberry, who assured him that Trevor is being held at an undisclosed location.

As far as the other employees of Flanagan Furniture, thirty-seven according to payroll records grudgingly provided by Trevor's Director of Information Systems, they're off for Christmas. Many will find out next week that they no longer have jobs. One of them will be the Information Systems guy himself. He's tried hard this morning to ingratiate himself to us, but Grady has seen a much different side. Michael has already contacted several search firms looking for potential replacements.

"Let's get things started," I say, as I pick up the agenda. "The first item is reorganization of the company leadership." I point out for the sake of the minutes that I currently control seventy percent of the company, while the other thirty percent is in Trevor's hands. "Let the record show that Trevor Stanley is not in attendance." It's duly noted, and we begin plowing through our business. My appointment as Company President is unanimously approved by me, then we move on to employees. Thirty-two of Trevor's thirty-seven employees are given pink slips. The Director of Information Systems, who has been lurking just outside the conference room, spews a choice line of invective before two off-duty Bradenton police officers escort him to his office to retrieve his personal effects. He's just forfeited the severance package we'd planned for him. I have to admit that one feels good.

One of the five employees we retain is Richie, our long-time union shop foreman who has been reduced to menial repair work. He'll be happy to hear that we'll soon be firing up the old factory floor and hiring craftsmen to work alongside him. Others who will be invited to stay include our secretary, I mean Executive Assistant, Ashton, two custodians Grady knows and trusts, and an assistant bookkeeper named Burnett who Grady hired soon after I left and has somehow held on through Trevor's regime. There will be another six or seven hirings in the coming weeks, but nothing like the bloated organizational chart Trevor had constructed.

Those who are being let go will be given three months' severance. This decision will make for some tenuous weeks ahead financially, but it's the way we do things. Like the aforementioned Director of Information Systems, Victor Ballentine won't be getting a dime, nor will he need it where he's likely to wind up after his cases snake through the court system.

The rest of the morning is much less eventful. A realtor recommends we put the new addition on the market and feels she can have a buyer within the month. The rest of the details begin to fall in line, and by eleven-twenty we're down to one item of business. I remove a single sheet of handwritten notes from the pocket of my seersucker, smooth it on the conference table, and wait while Lawyer Lawrence distributes formal copies to the others. I give them a few moments to read it over. Michael is finished first. He looks up and smiles. His dream is becoming reality. Grady gets teary-eyed.

I begin reading. "According to the partnership plan we drew up when I made Trevor and Grady shareholders, Flanagan Furniture reserves the right to repurchase the shares at an amount in accordance with the company's most recent end-of-year financial statements. Once the new addition is sold, a portion of those proceeds will be used to buy out Trevor's share."

It's an expense, a big expense, that I wish we could avoid, but having Trevor lording over the company, even from prison, will stunt its future growth and direction. It'll be better this way.

"Effective once the property sale is completed, the company will be divided into ownership shares as follows." I consult my notes just in case my memory trips me up.

"Grady, you've been my friend for longer than anyone. You came here in the beginning and stayed loyal through the early years. I counted on you and you never let me down. Life became difficult a few years ago, and you had to sell your stake in the company. I want you to have back your fifteen percent share of the company that you helped build." I look at Lawyer Lawrence and say, "Please make this happen as quickly as possible."

Grady's still weepy. I wish he would get a handle on that before he makes me start crying, too. I move on.

"My daughter, Stephanie, will have a four percent share of the company."

Maybe not a great decision, but the right decision. At

least I'll be providing some stability in her future. She and Randy won't have the kind of money that allows them to chase their hairbrained schemes and get-rich quick ideas, but it's something. It's time to move on.

"Michael, I couldn't be happier that you're joining the company. Even when you were a small boy, I felt a bond between us. You're a talented and thoughtful young man, just as I hoped you would be. Your share of the company will be fifty-one percent. It's a lot for a young man, but my dream of the company staying in our family remains alive because of you. I love you and want you to do great things."

Now there's not a dry eye in the place. We're ripping tissues from the box at a hectic pace. Poor Ashton has had to stop taking notes to wipe her eyes.

And I'm not done yet. I check my watch and find it's eleven-thirty. Claire should've arrived to pick me up by now. That was my plan. I ask Ashton to see if she's here. While she's out we take a quick break. I'm drinking from the water fountain in the waiting area when I see her come in.

"Done?" she asks.

"Almost. Just a couple more minutes. Come in."

Claire demurs, but I insist. She takes a seat off to the side, away from the conference table. I insist she move to the seat formerly occupied by the realtors and others we've called upon this morning. She reluctantly does, and I get things rolling again.

"Just to recap, Grady holds a fifteen percent share of the company, Stephanie has four percent, and Michael has fifty-one."

"That leaves thirty percent," Lawyer Lawrence says.

"The clarity I've experienced the past couple weeks has

been a gift from God," I say. "I've never been much of a believer, but how else can you explain it?"

No one answers, but I didn't think they would. This is my show.

"One reason I was given a second chance was to make amends for the way I treated Claire. Her life has been difficult since she and I had a relationship many years ago. I saw some of that back when I was still working here, but never did anything to help her. Today I'm going to make that right." I pause, glance at my notes, then say, "Claire will have a thirty percent share of Flanagan Furniture. It is hers to do with as she wishes."

I look down the table at her and smile.

"I feel Claire can help keep alive the values and ideals that I hold near and dear to my heart. Though our time together has been considerably less than with others in my life, she's as much a part of me as my arms and legs. In fact, she's more than arms or legs. She's my heart."

I pause to let this sink in, then say to Michael, Grady, and Claire, "Look at your partners. Together you're going to return this company to its past excellence." I pat Grady on the arm. "Grady, will you accept the position of Company President?"

"I would be humbled and honored."

"Michael, will be our Sales Manager and Chairman of the Board of Directors?"

"I can't wait to get started, Grandpa."

"And, dear Claire?"

Her eyes are glistening. "Yes, darling?"

I leave my seat, make my way past Michael and Lawyer Lawrence, get on my knee in front of her, and ask, "Will you be my wife?"

She says yes and my world is perfect.

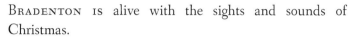

BRADENTON IS alive with the sights and sounds of Christmas.

I've heard people say they don't understand how you can get in the Christmas spirit in a place where there are palm trees and temperatures in the seventies.

Who are they kidding?

Claire and I enjoy lunch at one of those foo-foo places she likes so much. She tried to talk me into one of my old haunts, a diner or pizza place, but I only want what she wants, so we do foo-foo. Next we stop by a jewelry shop on Manatee Avenue, a place that has commissioned several of its display cases from our company. I tell the guy behind the counter to show us the good stuff. He lights up, then pulls out a tray of wedding rings with five figure prices on them.

"We don't have money for something that pricey," Claire insists. I smile and wave my company credit card. She still talks me down to a ring with a four-figure price tag. Sensible Claire. She'll be good watching over the company if I ever lose clarity.

Our next stop is the Rock and Redeemer Church. The parking lot is empty, other than one car that I recognize from yesterday. We find the front door locked, but a side door has a buzzer on it, so we ring. Pastor Lonnie opens it and seems delighted that we've returned. He mentions nothing about yesterday.

"Christmas Eve service is at seven," he says. "You're early."

He invites us in, and we tell him everything. And I do mean everything. Our relationship years ago, Claire's failed marriage, my condition, and everything we've been through the past couple weeks. We end by telling him we're getting married tomorrow.

"If we have too much baggage," I say. "If you'd prefer not to, we'll understand, but we would like you to marry us."

Pastor Lonnie rocks back and forth in his office chair as he laughs. There's something funny about seeing the little man's body shaking about, so we start laughing, too.

"Tell me the time and place."

We do, then he asks us to pray with him, and during that prayer I feel something I've never felt before. I wish I could describe it but can't. Its contentment mixed with excitement and a little bit of awe. Maybe there's some magic in there, too. I have no doubt that God exists and that He knows Claire and me. He knows we've made mistakes along the way, but He loves us anyway. I hug Pastor Lonnie. He tells me he loves me, and I tell him that I love him back. He invites us to return in a couple hours for Christmas Eve services, but we turn him down.

"We have a bit of shopping to do," I explain. He smiles and wishes us well.

AFTER RUNNING by the house and switching out Claire's nice car for my old Riviera we head for a Christmas tree stand next to a pawn shop on Tamiami Trail. I drive. It's the first time Claire's ridden with me, and if I'm scaring her, she does a good job of hiding it.

"Look," I call out gleefully as we pull into the pothole-laden lot. "Half-price."

Who would have expected it? A Christmas tree sale on Christmas Eve. Then we start looking through the selection and understand why. They're the misfits and castoffs of the tree world. Evergreens with bald patches, brown spots, and other imperfections. I'm ready to give up and head for Home Depot for an artificial tree, but Claire is adamant.

"We need our own tree. A *real* tree. Not that artificial one you and Rosalie used all those years."

Twenty minutes later we're pulling away from the lot. Our seven-foot kinked trunk bald-spotted, green-on-it's-way-to-brown spruce tree is tied to the top of the Riviera.

"It has imperfections," Claire declares. "Just like us."

Since we're starting fresh, we run by Walmart to get decorations. One look at the lines surrounding that place and we're back on the road. Then, I have an idea.

"Let's pull in here," I say.

"It's a second-hand store."

"I came here the day I walked away from Pinehurst Pavilion." I hold up my left foot, the one not holding down the gas pedal. "I got these for next to nothing."

Bingo. There are plenty of decorations for sale, many dinged and tarnished. They'll be perfect with our tree. I let Claire take the wheel on the way back to my place. I'm starting to feel a headache coming on and hope I can remain clear long enough to decorate our tree. It's quite an effort to get the thing through the door, so I sit down on the sofa for a few moments while Claire gets me a glass of water. It's six-forty. Christmas Eve. The night before my wedding day. I can't wait.

CHAPTER EIGHTEEN
CHRISTMAS DAY

I awaken and know exactly where I am.

Alone.

The bed next to me hasn't been slept in.

In the distance I hear music.

Christmas music.

Hark the Herald Angels Sing.

It sounds beautiful. I close my eyes, lie back, and let it wash over me.

Then, a thought. Oh no, am I dead?

That's ridiculous. I'm not dead. I'm in my own bed at my own house. It's Christmas Day. Claire must've turned on the old stereo in the living room. There used to be several Christmas albums in there. That has to be it.

It's Christmas.

And our wedding day.

"Thank you, God," I utter under my breath as I throw off the covers. It's six-fifty-five. The bedroom windows are open, allowing a gentle northerly breeze to pass through. The sky is brightening in the East, promising a picture-perfect day. The kind a guy hopes for when he's marrying the love of his life.

In the hallway outside the bedroom I find Claire pushing boxes of Christmas decorations. The old ones, mine and Rosalie's.

"Are you okay with me returning these to the attic?" I'm getting the living room ready."

"Let me take them up." I do, then join her downstairs. The new misfit Christmas tree we selected together looks perfect. What a wonderful job she's done. We kiss in front of the tree, then enjoy bowls of Raisin Bran with orange juice.

"Where did you sleep?" I ask.

"The little room in back."

"Don't do that again."

"I won't have to. After today we'll be married."

I find her little demonstration of pre-wedding propriety to be humorous and touching. I can tell by looking around that she's cleaned from top to bottom. The wood floors give off the pleasing scent of Murphy's Oil Soap. She's placed air fresheners in outlets in the living and dining rooms. The scent is evergreen. Perfect.

"Do we need any chairs?" I ask as I inspect the house. "There are some folding chairs in the garage."

"We have seating for five on the sofa and two chairs. That will take care of everyone."

By everyone Claire means Grady, Michael, Pastor Lonnie's wife, our new executive assistant, Ashton, and her husband, Carlos. Ashton practically begged to be included, and since their families live in Texas, we happily said yes.

Grady arrives first, at nine, an hour before the ceremony.

"Who gets married at ten in the damn morning?" he grouses good naturedly as he pours a cup of coffee.

"People like me do," I answer. "People whose days tend to end around six. Ten is already the middle of the day."

Claire and I excuse ourselves to get ready. I'm not allowed to see the bride before the ceremony, so she goes to the back room and I go to my bedroom. I choose a white seersucker. It looks snazzy if I do say so myself. Down below I can hear the sound of footsteps moving around the house and the occasional peal of laughter. Our guests are starting to arrive.

At five before ten, Grady comes up to get me. "Let's get this show on the road, brother," he says as he checks me out. I love this man and can't think of anyone else I would rather have standing next to me. It's hard to believe that just a couple weeks ago he was considering ending his life. I'm glad I've been able to provide some support.

We head down the stairs and as the living room comes into view, I'm shocked by what I see.

It's packed. With people.

I look at Grady, who's wearing a smile that goes from ear to ear. "You?" I ask.

He nods.

Pastor Lonnie is standing in front of the Christmas tree. He waves when we make eye contact. I spot his much-taller wife off to one side. She's standing next to my daughter, Stephanie. We gaze at one another and I find myself forgetting the animosity between us. Then I look at Randy standing just behind her. Warming up to him will take a bit longer, but I still appreciate his coming.

The left side of the living room is wall-to-wall lawyers. Our new company lawyer, Lawrence, is holding hands with a stunningly beautiful young woman who has to be his wife.

I do a double take when I spot Ripley Snodgrass, the number two guy for Trevor's legal team. The guy must be a really decent human being. In the back, barely visible, is Kiara Kennedy. She winks.

The FBI is well represented on the other side of the room. Agents Cruz, Hatcher, and Hockenberry are out of the Bureau's standard issue attire and look like normal folks. Cruz has a woman with him. Hockenberry has a gentleman. Hatcher came alone. Executive Assistant Ashton and her guy are crowded into a corner but seem happy just to be here.

That's fifteen people, not counting whoever is seated on the couch. I crane my neck and can see the back of Michael's head. And next to him, seated in the middle of the sofa like the Queen herself, FBI Director Gwendolyn Abbott-Newsome. She waves and I think I might be dreaming.

And as good as it all is, it only gets better. I shake a few hands, receive a couple pats on the back, and warm hugs from Kiara, Agent Hockenberry, and Director Newsome. Stephanie kisses my cheek and seems to want to say something. I stop her. "I'm so glad you're here, sweetheart. I love you."

As we take our positions Michael goes to the old stereo, the same one Claire was playing Christmas music on this morning. He puts a record on and lays the needle in place. I'm surprised he knows how to use it, really. It's a scratchy version of the Wedding March, played at a painstakingly slow thirty-three rotations per minute instead of the forty-five a single record is made for. Michael blushes, shrugs, and looks around for help. It's Director Newsome who comes to his rescue, speeding up the record, and accepting a short round of applause. This is a happy group of people. Despite being pulled away from their homes and, in some cases, their families, they're happy to be celebrating this day with Claire and me. I love them for it.

When I see heads turning toward the stairway, I follow their gaze and see the most beautiful, most heavenly, most anticipated vision of my life. My forever companion, for as long as forever might be for us, my radiant, lovely, sexy Claire. Nothing can diminish the vision of her as she makes her way toward me. Not the scratchy record, not the sound of Grady's stomach growling, not even Randy's whispering to Stephanie, "Can you believe they found a midget preacher?" I look at Randy just long enough to mouth, "He's not a midget, he's a mighty man of God," then return my gaze to Claire. She reaches the bottom of the stairs, makes the turn, and a few moments later we're together.

I wish I could remember everything Pastor Lonnie said. I wish I had taken time to gaze into the happy faces of our guests. The fact is, my eyes never strayed from my wife. And afterward we accept the congratulations and well-wishes of people who care enough to come from far and wide. Someone has arranged for a post-ceremony luncheon. Chinese food, a Christmas tradition on a day that most restaurants close their doors. The food arrives in those little boxes you expect from Chinese restaurants. Stephanie steps up and places the food on the kitchen table, along with paper plates and utensils, and we dig in. People fill their plates and find places around the kitchen and living room to stand and eat. The conversation is loud, and there's plenty of laughter. I see Director Newsome chatting with Ripley Snodgrass and Kiara Kennedy, and it makes me happy that people from different sides of our lives can find something to talk about.

Then, just after noon, they start to find their way to the front door. There are planes to catch and family dinners to make. No one seems rushed, nor do they seem intent on staying long. That's fine. I want to spend time with my beautiful Claire. The last to leave is Grady. He cleans up the kitchen a bit, shakes my hand, hugs Claire, and says, "You know where I am if you need anything."

"Don't worry, Grady," I say. "We can handle it from here."

A HONEYMOON SHOULD BE sweet and satisfying. Love should be made, and deep conversations should be enjoyed. The future should be discussed. The past should be reminisced. One's thoughts and joys and wishes should be centered only on their mate. The outside world should cease to exist.

That describes our day together. Perfect in every way.

The sky outside has grown dark. Neither of us has looked at a clock, lost as we've been in each other. I hold my Claire close, kiss her forehead, and say, "I love you."

She tells me she loves me, too.

"I can't wait for tomorrow," I say softly.

"I can't wait for all of our tomorrows," she responds.

It's perfect. Just perfect.

CHAPTER NINETEEN
SATURDAY, DECEMBER 26

I awaken and wonder where I am.

The place isn't one I've seen before.

Or is it?

I hear someone talking. They sound far away.

PART THREE

CHAPTER TWENTY

THERE'S LIGHT COMING IN THROUGH THE BLINDS AT the end of the bed where I'm staying.

Somewhere outside my room, a door opens, then closes. I hear steps on stairs, then a man much older than me pokes his head in. "Got time for a visitor?"

"Only for a little bit. I have to get to work."

He comes in. I think I know him, but maybe not. He pulls up a chair. I sit up on the edge of the bed. He talks for a long time, but I don't know who he is or what he's talking about, so eventually I tell him it's time to leave. He goes.

THE PHONE next to the chair in my room rings several times. I pick it up.

"Flanagan Furniture. Can I help you?"

"Grandpa, it's Michael."

"Michael! How are you?"

"I'm doing great. We're so busy out here. I want to tell you all about it sometime."

"I'd love to hear about it. How's your lacrosse team doing? That's what you call it, right? Lacrosse?"

Michael doesn't say anything for a moment, and I'm afraid we've been disconnected.

"Are you still there? Michael?"

"Yes, Grandpa, I just wanted to say hello."

"Tell your Mom I'm going to try to get up to visit her this month, will you, son?"

THE DOOR to the room where I'm staying opens, and I'm overjoyed.

It's my Claire.

I hold out my hand and say, "Come here, darling."

She smiles and comes to me. She's holding a little cake. Not one of those full-sized ones you get at the bakery, but a smaller one.

"Is that coconut?" I ask.

"It is. Your favorite."

She sets it down on the table at the foot of the bed, takes a knife from her apron, and slices two pieces. She puts them on plates and hands me one.

"Thank you, Claire. What's the big occasion?"

"Our first anniversary, my love. Happy Anniversary to us." She takes a bite of cake. I do the same.

"So, it's our anniversary?" I ask, my mouth full of delicious cake. "How long?"

She answers, but I don't know what she says. I can't take my eyes off her. She's older than I remember, but no less beautiful. She moves with grace and loves me completely. I love her, too.

"I love you," I say.

Claire says something back, but I don't know what.

AUTHOR'S NOTE

People sometimes ask me if there is any truth behind specific events and places in my books. In a word, yes! Plenty of the places and lesser events are real. For example, in the book you've just read, there are plenty of real-life references. Here are a few:

Clear Christmas takes place in **Bradenton, Florida**. That's where we live. While Neal's address is fictional, many of the other locations and landmarks are real. Robin says you need to try the stone crab claws at **Star Fish Company** that Grady loves so much. I'm a big fan of the sub sandwiches at **Publix**. Longboat Key, Anna Maria Island, Cortez Road, and Manatee Avenue are all real – and busy, especially in the winter.

As a kid who was crazy about the NBA, I loved watching Neal's favorite player, **Nate Thurmond,** battle the Bullet's Wes Unseld for rebounds. Both were terribly underrated.

In 1979, **Disney World** tickets really were $6.50. Look it up! Our family visited soon after they opened, in the winter of 1972. Tickets were $3.75 then. I loved *Mr. Toad's Wild Ride*. Mom preferred *It's a Small World*.

Clear Christmas is FBI Director **Gwendolyn Abbott-Newsome's** third book. She started in *The Resurrection of Hucklebuck Jones* as a spoiled young girl who matured into a tenacious attorney. She ascended to FBI Director in *Some Summer*. I like her.

I'm not above slipping a few real names into my books. This time I called out my buddy, cat litter salesman extraordinaire **Jim Ingram**, who often uses the line, "Not my monkey, not my circus." It's fun to use the names of people I like and respect.

As for everything else, I just made it up.

So, there you go.

ACKNOWLEDGMENTS

To everyone who read my previous books, thank you! Clear Christmas is my seventh!

Thanks to my editor Judy Falin Dellinger.

I appreciate my beta readers! You continue to come through.

I love my family. A special shout-out to my Mom and Dad who are in their eighties and handling COVID like champs.

Robin makes my world go around.

And thank you, Lord, for giving me the time, interest, and ability to write these words. Without you, I'm nothing.

Cover Design: SelfPubBookCovers.com/RLSather

Made in the USA
Columbia, SC
02 December 2020

26080384R00159